Case for Sergeant Beef

Case for Sergeant Beef

By

LEO BRUCE

ACADEMY
CHICAGO
LIMITED

Copyright ©Leo Bruce 1951

First American Edition 1980 Academy Chicago Ltd.

Published by Academy Chicago
425 North Michigan Avenue
Chicago, Illinois 60611

Printed and bound in the United States of America.

First paperback edition 1981 Academy Chicago

Library of Congress Cataloging in Publication Data

Croft-Cooke, Rupert, 1903-1980
    Case for Sergeant Beef.

    Reprint of the 1975 ed. published by I. Henry
Publications, Hornchurch, Eng.
    I.   Title.
PR6005.R673C3   1980   823'.912   80-20038
ISBN 0-89733-037-4
ISBN 0-89733-036-6 (pbk.)

CONTENTS

CHAPTER ONE

By Way of Preamble

I HAD made up my mind to have no more to do with murder. Before the war I had faithfully chronicled the investigations of Sergeant Beef into five mysteries and had enjoyed watching him, whose great quality as a detective was his sturdy common sense, find his way among the maze of evidence and eventually, and always, get his man.

When I had first met him he had been no more than a village policeman, and it was my ability to record his work in a series of novels which had raised him to the level of a famous investigator. But he had shown little or no gratitude and had frequently complained that the books I had written about him were not widely enough read. So now that the war was over and I had decided to abandon the work of a crime novelist for the more secure and profitable profession of marine insurance, I had no scruple in telling him so. He had never appreciated me, I felt, and I wondered whom he would find to replace me as his Boswell.

Whoever it might be would have no easy job. For Beef, burly, red-faced, heavy of hand and humour, with that dark ginger moustache of his which straggled over his lips and looked as though its tips were nourished on beer, with his portentous announcements and his irritating complacency, was not a man to appeal to the great public as an inspired investigator. And although I had to admit that he always *did* find the answer where others failed, and that under his solid exterior there was something akin to genius, and that he had a kind of boyish enthusiasm which was very infectious, still I rather wondered whether he would find another writer to take him up. The fashion was for detectives of high social standing and large private incomes, while Beef was dependent on what he actually earned in his cases.

At any rate, I had had enough. It is true that I had not

seen *very* much bloodshed during the war, though as an officer in the R.I.A.S.C. I had been, as they say, not a thousand miles from the fighting, but still I felt I wanted a rest from murder, and I decided to tell Beef frankly that if he intended to return to detection he would have to find a replacement for me.

I had heard from him once or twice during the war. He had joined the Special Investigation Branch of the Corps of Military Police, and had doubtless had his little successes in tracing missing stores, examining questionable imprest returns and arresting officers who had written phoney cheques. I was prepared to find him just as pleased with himself as ever. And I set off on the afternoon of New Year's Day to see him, break the news of my new profession, and wish him luck in finding my successor.

His home he had found before the war when he had first retired from the Force, and was lucky enough still to possess intact. I smiled as I remembered his first search for it, and his insistence that it must be near Baker Street, which he described as the Harley Street of detection.

'Never do to be out of the swim,' he said, and when he had settled in his house in Lilac Crescent he had stuck up an absurd brass plate with *W. Beef: Investigations* on it in giant letters. I was not surprised to find this in its place, and freshly polished, when I reached his house that day.

He opened the door himself and greeted me with his big slow grin.

'Hullo,' he said. 'I was wondering when you'd turn up. Come along in. And a happy New Year!'

He led the way to what he always called his 'front room', a place of Spanish mahogany, sentimental engravings, and an atmosphere in which the stale smoke of Beef's pipes blended with the last meal eaten at the plush-covered table.

Beef pointed to a horse-hair chair for me and slowly lowered himself into his own favourite one, then lit his pipe.

'I suppose you've come round to see if there's anything doing in the way of a murder story for you to write?" he grinned.

I explained rather tartly that I had come for nothing of the sort, that I had quite made up my mind to have nothing more to do with detection.

'That's all right,' he said, as though I had been apologizing. 'I can soon get someone else to write up my cases. I shouldn't be surprised but what it mightn't be just as well, all things considered.'

'What exactly do you mean by that?' I asked icily.

'Well, you never made much of a success of it, did you? Not to say *success*,' he added.

'I don't understand you, Beef,' I retorted. 'When I met you you were a village policeman. *I* turned you into a famous detective. I wrote each of your cases.'

'But who worked them out?' asked Beef with a triumphant grin. 'Who found the answers?'

'I'm not denying that you did. But you should understand that it's no use being a good detective nowadays unless you've got someone to write you up. Publicity's the thing.'

'That's what I say,' said Beef. 'And I want someone who'll give it me. I solve the mysteries, don't I? Have I ever failed? I ask you. And some of them have been pretty tricky and left the Yard wondering. But what do I get? A few copies of your books in the lending libraries. My wife's sister who's always reading, always got her nose in a book she has, says that the young lady at the library she goes to has never heard of Sergeant Beef. What do you think of that?'

I was too angry to speak at first. Then I said ironically – 'I suppose *I'm* to blame?'

''*Course* you are,' said Beef. 'Why, I ought to be right up with the top-notchers now. Lord Simon Plimsoll and M. Amer Picon and them. I get at the truth just as clever. don't I?'

'You may,' I admitted. 'But you lack the polish, Beef. These modern detectives are mostly related to Dukes, or if not they *know* everyone. They're welcomed in the best houses. They're always invited to those house-parties at which all the best murders happen. Not to put too fine a point on it, Beef, you're crude. Rough and ready. Bourgeois.'

'Now you're coming to it!' said Beef. 'That's why I'm not as famous as the rest, is it? Class distinction, again. Well, if that's the case it's your fault. You ought never to have made me out no more than what I was. Suppose you'd written me up as Lord William Beef. What then? We'd have had them reading fit to bust themselves.'

'Please don't be nonsensical,' I said, for I saw the satisfied grin on his red face.

'What I need is someone to take me seriously,' he said. 'It's no good you trying to make people see I'm a great detective if you're giving them a laugh half the time.'

'I write about things as I see them,' I said.

'Literary conscience, eh?' laughed Beef. 'All I can say is it doesn't pay.'

'At any rate, you needn't worry any more,' I said bitterly. 'You are certainly at liberty to find someone else to record any further cases you may get. Someone who'll present you as slim and aristocratic, with a keen eye and excellently cut clothes, if you like. I'm going to do other work.'

'Well, that's your business. I dare say it will pay you better. You're not really cut out for writing, are you?'

I treated this with silent scorn.

'Not according to some of the reviewers you're not, anyway,' concluded Beef. 'Still, it's a pity in a way, particularly just now.'

'Why just now?' I could not help asking.

'Because there's a lady calling round presently with what looks like a nice little case. A very nice little case.'

'I couldn't be less interested,' I said, using, rather effectively, I thought, some of the idiom I had learnt in the army.

'No? Well, that's all right. Because if this case is what I think of it, it's serious. Nasty. Murder, or suicide that's been forced on a man to make it almost murder in itself. And I want to get at the truth with no larking about.'

'Are you inferring that I have ever done any "larking about", as you call it, while we have been investigating?'

'No, but the way you've told the story anybody would

think that I had. This case is serious. It wants serious handling. So perhaps it's just as well that you're not going to
write it up. Still, you may as well stay and have a cup of tea.'

Frankly I did not know what to do.

'What is her name?' I asked Beef.

'Whose name?'

'The name of the lady who's coming to see you.'

'Miss Shoulter.'

It meant nothing to me. I had not been studying the
news of crime in newspapers lately.

'She's the sister of a man found dead in a wood in Kent
last week,' said Beef.

'Sounds pretty commonplace.'

'Well, what do you expect? Frills on? He was dead, wasn't
he? Shot with a 12-bore. Half his head shot away. What
more do you want?'

I was about to say that I wanted nothing except to start
my daily work in a quiet office. But at that moment the
front-door bell rang and Beef went out to return a moment
later with Miss Shoulter.

'This is Mr Townsend,' he said, 'who does the clerical side
of my work. Miss Shoulter.'

I was furious, but I managed to conceal it as I shook
hands with Beef's client.

She was a horse-faced woman in her forties. Really horse-
faced. It was impossible to look at her without thinking of
stables. And she wore the kind of severe tweeds and shapeless felt hat which went with her equine features. She sat on
a straight chair, accepted a cigarette from me, and began to
talk in a loud, cheerful voice.

'I want you,' she said, 'to investigate the death of my
brother. The fools think it was suicide.'

'What fools?'

'Everyone. I'm told you're more competent than you look.
The police will do nothing, and I won't have one of these
pansified snobs who are supposed to be brilliant investigators hanging around. You can count on me for your fees
and expenses. And you can bring your boy-friend with

you.' She gave me a jerk of her head. 'Only you must get cracking.'

'I think I ought to explain ...' I began.

But Beef boomed out before I could finish.

'No need for explanations now,' he said. 'I'll take the case. Now what's the address?'

So against my better judgement, against all my resolutions, I found myself back in the world of crime, found myself following Beef down to Barnford in Kent, and once more watching while he set about the elucidation of a mystery. And a mystery it really looked.

CHAPTER TWO

Journal of Wellington Chickle

ABOUT a year earlier Mr Wellington Chickle had begun to write his Journal. This Journal is now one of Sergeant Beef's most prized souvenirs, though it only came into his hands long after the Shoulter Case was concluded, and no one knew of its existence, still less had any access to it, while the investigation was proceeding. It is an astonishing document written in large curious handwriting, full of flourishes so ornamental and detailed that they are almost like the illuminated capitals of an old manuscript. It is clear at a glance that the man who wrote it loved his work and probably had nothing to do but perfect it. The Journal opens in March 1945. Its first entry gives the key to the whole thing.

First Entry

I have decided to commit a murder. And before I go any farther I want to try to give my reasons for this as accurately as possible. They will be so very important to the psychologist of the future when the Wellington Chickle Murder Case has taken its right place as one of the great historical crimes, when such names as Crippen and Landru will be obscure in comparison with my name. Not, of course, that my name will be associated with the crime during my lifetime. After I have finished my days in peace this Journal will be given to the world and then for the first time it will be realized that the brains of Scotland Yard have been outmatched by the genius of one who seemed no more than a sober, gentle, retired watchmaker.

The reasons, then. But again I must digress to explain what are *not* the reasons. I shall not commit murder for gain, for revenge, for love, for the sake of brutality, for escape from a blackmailer or bully, for spite, for hatred or as a protest against anything whatsoever. In fact – and this is the very crux of the matter – *I shall have no motive*. And because I shall have no motive I shall never be found out. In other words my murder will be art for art's sake, murder merely and entirely for the sake of murder. It sounds simple. So do all great ideas.

I am perfectly sane, of course. I am considered rather a nice old gentleman, fond of books and gardening and devoted to children. A hundred people could testify to my sanity. I am not even an eccentric or a solitary. I am generally liked, even respected.

So my reasons are these. I am going to commit a murder because I have found the key to successful murder – to have no discoverable motive. Because I want to achieve something before I die which will make my rather odd name live in the annals of time, and murder seems the surest way of achieving this. Because I really have nothing much to do with the remaining years of my life, no absorbing interest, and I think that the planning and carrying out of this will give me what I need. Because I think that there's too much fuss made about life and death and cannot see that it matters that death should come to one man or woman a few years before it would normally have happened. Because it will be fascinating to watch the police blundering in all the wrong directions, and to know that I, and I alone, am aware of the truth. And because I remember, fifty years ago, a schoolmaster saying to me in class that I should never set the Thames on fire, never amount to anything much, never achieve anything worth while; and if I were to die now it would be in the knowledge that he was right, whereas if I carry out my plan and do what so many others have failed to do and commit a successful and undetected murder I shall know that I have proved him a hundred times wrong.

So that is *why* I am going to do it. And as time goes by I shall make up my mind where, how, when, and to whom it shall be done. I shall not hurry these decisions. I shall take my time to think, to plan, to ensure absolute success. Even the thought of the great day, towards which I am already looking eagerly, on which I can say that I have done it, that

I have achieved the all-but-impossible, shall not cause me to rush or scamp my preparations. It is said that a murderer always makes one mistake. I shall be the exception. I shall make no mistake.

Second Entry

It is a week since I wrote the above. I have decided not to put dates in this Journal, but to let it be a more or less continuous narrative. It will be easier to read like that. Not that it will in any case lack eager readers, for to know the truth at last about a mystery which has baffled the world for years will be incentive enough to scan even duller stories. And to the psychologist this could not be dull. Think, my friend, you are looking into the mind of Wellington Chickle, the man who beat detection, the coolest and most brilliant murderer of the century. You have the chance to study and analyse a brain more complex than that of a great poet or statesman. Do you not realize your good fortune?

So I will make it a straightforward story. And I start with this premise. Murder without motive, if a few simple precautions are taken, is a problem impossible to solve. If a man of good character waited in a suitably lonely spot and murdered *the first person who came along*, his guilt would never be suspected. Why? Because even if he shouted and called a dozen witnesses and so was known to have been on the scene of the crime, there would be nothing to connect him with it. Motive is *always* the connecting link. Always. So my first resolution is to murder someone I don't know, someone in whose death I could not possibly have any interest. That will not be difficult.

The next thing is to find the place. What a huge advantage I have over other mere slaves in the art of murder. They, poor fellows, are tied down by necessities. Where their victims are their crimes must be. They must, either by artificial means — and everything artificial is easily discovered — bring their victim to the spot, or choose a spot to which their victim goes. For me there are no such limitations. I choose my spot from the wide map of the earth and wait for the first arrival. And in case I am seen I give myself a good everyday reason for being in that spot. Too easy, once I have the crucial idea.

Now I remember many years ago during a walking tour in Kent finding a village called Barnford. It was a pleasant village with oldish red-brick houses and a square church tower. And near it was a wood through which ran a public footpath. I have been thinking that this will make the ideal spot. Lonely, but one could be sure of someone coming along sooner or later. Plenty of cover, before and after. The body to be found quickly if one wanted it found quickly, or not for a long time, if one wanted it concealed. And the sort of area in which I might well be living in the unlikely event of my having to give an account of myself. I shall go down there to-morrow and prospect.

Third Entry

I have been luckier than I could have hoped. I found an empty bungalow at Barnford, right on the outskirts of Dead-man's Wood. (Yes, that is actually its name. Is it not appropriate? I could scarcely repress a smile when I heard it!) The bungalow is called 'Labour's End', which again is very fitting, as I said quite truthfully that I wanted to retire and grow roses. The soil, I am told, is splendid for them. I have bought the little place not too expensively – I am in any case not perturbed by the outlay as I shall certainly stay there even after the Great Event. It will be pleasant in my declining years to visit the scene of my triumph.

I shall have a few neighbours. On the other side of the wood lives a Miss Shoulter who breeds spaniels – far enough away, I learn, for their yelping to be inaudible. And in the wood itself there is a larger house in which a family named Flipp lives. But they have their own way in from the road and do not use the footpath I remembered.

That footpath is just as I hoped – a narrow rather winding track between the trees which cuts right across the wood from near Miss Shoulter's bungalow to mine. I could be walking along it at any time of day or night without arousing the faintest suspicion, even on the night of a murder. Yet it is lonely enough to provide a dozen points at which the thing could be done, and done in the confidence that there were no witnesses. Ideal. I hope to move in next week.

Fourth Entry

I am comfortably established at Labour's End. It is really a very pleasant little house overlooking a sweep of country only cut by the railway line nearly a mile away. I have brought my own furniture down after it had been in store three years, since, in fact, I sold my business.

Mentioning that reminds me that I should give some account of myself, for when the facts about my murder come out after my death, it is certain that there will be a good deal of research into my past and the results may not be accurate. I want the true facts to be known.

I was an only son. My father was employed by a firm of stonemasons, and spent his life in chipping at memorial crosses for people who deserved no memorial. He was, by the standards of his time, well paid, and our little home in South London though dingy and cramped never knew the miseries of want or hunger.

I was given a better education than most sons of artisans and remained at school till I was nearly seventeen. Then I was apprenticed to an old watchmaker, a friend of my father, who taught me the trade which has served me ever since.

My father was an honest decent man, but an incurable sentimentalist with a taste for military history. He could reconstruct almost every battle fought by British armies and would bore his fellow customers in the saloon bar of the Mitre, which he 'used' for forty years, with detailed accounts of Waterloo or the Nile, until they told him to come off it. It was this passion of his which caused him to name me after the Iron Duke, and it was an unfortunate choice considering our curious surname. And when I failed to grow above five feet four inches it seemed even more out of place. However, both my father and my mother, a plump easy-going woman who took me to chapel on Sundays, delighted in it, never abbreviated it and could be heard shouting 'Wellington!' down our back-garden when they wanted me to come indoors.

At twenty-five I started my own watchmaking business in what was then a little town separated from London by open country, but which became, I'm glad to say, one of the busiest suburbs. My little shop thrived, and a quarter of a century later, when I was employing a dozen men and women and had a fine establishment, I sold it at the top of the market and retired on the proceeds, together with my not inconsiderable investments.

I forgot to say that I married at thirty a girl who brought me the initial capital I needed for enlarging my business. She failed to bear me a child and died some years before I retired.

Since I sold the shop I have been living in rooms, waiting for a chance to settle in the country.

That is my uneventful story and from it you will see, perhaps, why I have made up my mind to distinguish myself now. The man who bought my business has already changed the name, so that unless I achieve my great ambition no one twenty years hence will have heard of Wellington Chickle. But I shall achieve it.

CHAPTER THREE

Journal of Wellington Chickle
Continued

Fifth Entry

I have been unpacking and arranging my books. It is a pleasant task, although my anxiety to get them all into place so that I can refer to them easily has made me overtire myself a little. My library consists entirely of criminology in all its forms and I have spent a great deal of money over many years in accumulating it. *Old Trials*, the *Newgate Calendar*, *Lives of the Highwaymen*, a formidable row of books on Criminal Jurisprudence, and everything that is worth while in modern detective fiction, from Poe and Gaboriau down to Bentley and Agatha Christie. I am really proud of some of the more unusual items, and get great amusement from dipping into the *Famous Trials* series and seeing the idiotic mistakes made by blundering murderers of the past. How little finesse most of them possessed. They approached the delicate matter of murder as though it were a pick and shovel job and allowed their passions to betray them into every kind of impatience and risk. I smile when I realize my superiority over that sort of violence, for in my crime there will be *no* passion and so no risk at all.

I took a walk along the footpath through Deadman's Wood to-day, and found it bright with bluebells. I should like my murder to be in spring, I think, while these beautiful blue flowers make a shining carpet underfoot. Only I should have to be careful of trampling them in any indicative way. However, I have not begun to consider such details yet. I am still concerned with the Place and I think I have found it. A fallen tree beside the path would give excellent concealment and it is roughly half-way through the wood at a point where the trees on either side are thickest. With tremendous inward excitement I decided to test the hiding-place behind that tree and to find out whether one could see a person approaching. I crouched down and peered over the trunk. Excellent. At dusk I should be quite invisible and should see anyone from at least twelve yards away. Exactly as I hoped.

My enjoyment was irritatingly interrupted by someone approaching from the *other* direction, and you may imagine my annoyance when I found it was the pasty-faced curate from Barnford walking alone through the wood. And he was tactless enough to smile when he saw me crouching there. Really it is a good thing for him that I have decided that my victim shall be *quite unknown to me,* for I could have killed him for his cheerful loquacity.

'How do you do?' he asked. He might as well have said, 'Dr Livingstone, I presume?'

'How d'you do?' I answered with assumed good humour.

'Picking bluebells?' he asked.

'I was just about to,' I said. 'Lovely, aren't they? As a Londoner I find your countryside most attractive.'

And what must he do but start a long conversation while I brushed the leaves and a little dirt from my clothes. He came from London too it appeared, from Sydenham to be precise. He had only been here two years and remembered his first spring in Kent, so he knew *just* how I felt. The fool. If he knew just how I felt he would know that I wanted to assassinate him for his smugness then and there.

And of course he turned the conversation to me. Where did I live? What was my name? Would I be attending his church?

To the last question I replied solemnly that indeed I should, every Sunday, for I realize that this will be an important part of the character I am creating for myself. A nice old church-going retired tradesman. *Not* chapel, I feel, and certainly not Roman Catholic. Too suggestive of earnestness or even violence. Church of England is the safest bet – so wholly non-committal and yet so thoroughly respectable. I invited the curate back to tea and flattered myself that I appeared delighted to watch him satisfying a phenomenal appetite. No wonder he has a pasty look, and that his ears are bright red. Constipation, undoubtedly.

Sixth Entry

Really, considering it's only about six weeks since I first began to make definite plans, I think I have done very well. I have found the district, and the very point in that district for my purpose. Though I had all the British Isles to choose from I am satisfied that the spot I have finally selected could not be better. And I have so arranged matters that I have a perfectly natural reason for being near that spot at any time of day or night. I *live* here. Not bad for so short a time.

I must now go on to consider the method, and I need scarcely say that I have been giving very careful thought to that. Poison is out of the question, for the thing must of course be spontaneous. Poison means endless preparation and precaution for the layman, endless risk in obtaining it, endless trouble in administering it, and endless difficulties in making it appear as suicide. Besides if I am to murder my man at that point in Deadman's Wood (how I *delight* in that name) poison is unthinkable. What would I be doing standing there offering prussic acid to a chance pedestrian? It's absurd.

Nor do I need to employ any of those elaborate death machines so popular in murder stories, poisoned darts blown from pipes, injections, or poisoned scratches, weights timed to drop on unsuspecting crania – these are all the inventions of less fortunate murderers who have to wipe out a certain person at a certain time and place, and establish their own alibis. All quite unnecessary for me.

Strangling and suffocation are 'out' too, if for no other reason than that of my inadequate height and strength. Drowning is of course out of the question, and such chancy things as bows-and-arrows or boomerangs I prefer not to consider. Then again I am not powerful enough for clubbing or smashing the head with some gardening tool like a spade, and an axe seems to me a clumsy weapon more suited to early warfare than to a brilliantly-planned twentieth-century murder.

This brings me to a choice of two classes of weapon, a blade or a firearm. Each has its advantages of course. The blade, whether sword, spear, knife, dagger, or razor, is silent, but the gun is sure. At least it will be in my hands. For twenty years the only relaxation I have known from the work of my shop has been a little rough shooting I have had in Essex. I hired it with an old friend called Whitman, and we would miss very few week-ends. With a good 12-bore on that path I could be as sure of my man as the hangman is of *his*. But of course, there's the noise, and the possession of a gun and many other factors. It will need a great deal of consideration.

Meanwhile Miss Shoulter has called – at least I suppose it was a call. I was working in my garden this afternoon when I heard what I took to be a man's voice shouting from the gate.

'Hullo! Are you Mr Chickle?'

I straightened up and saw a woman with a long sunburnt face and shapeless check tweeds standing there with two spaniel puppies on leads. I never forget my character as that of an amiable old gentleman, and walked across to her smiling in the most friendly way.

'I am, and you must be Miss Shoulter. Do come in.'

''Fraid I can't,' she yelled in that ear-splitting male voice of hers. 'Got the pups with me. Thought I'd just come and say hullo, as we're neighbours.'

'That's very good of you,' I smiled.

Then she kept me talking there for five minutes, though I was impatient to get back to my flower-bed. Maddening woman. Why should she think I am interested in her dogs? I asked her at last why she didn't breed retrievers.

'Why? Fond of shooting?' she said. Such a direct question. I was taken off my guard.

'No,' I said. Then I built up a bit more of my character. 'I couldn't bear to hurt live creatures,' I added.

'No need to do that,' she shouted. 'Been shooting all me

life and don't believe I've caused any pain. Not as much as nature causes with *her* ways of killing, anyway.'

'Do you do any shooting now?' I asked.

'Not much. I've got a couple of guns still.'

'Perhaps you feel that living alone ...' I began. But she gave a great vulgar hoarse laugh.

'Me? I can look after myself without guns,' she said. And looking at her I thought it only too likely to be true.

A minute later she was gone, leaving me quite a lot to think about.

Seventh Entry

I have engaged a housekeeper, an excellent woman named Mrs Pluck. I am paying her rather large wages, but she is more than worth it, for she is not only a splendid cook with a passion for keeping the house scrupulously clean, but she has what almost amounts to a mania for punctuality. Although she carries a wrist-watch her first request was for a kitchen alarm clock and she seems always to keep an eye on the time. This will one day serve my purpose, I feel sure. If I can depend on her to notice the times of my comings and goings the day will come when she will provide an alibi.

She is, I must admit, slightly forbidding in manner and appearance, nearly six feet in height and with a face that might justly be called gaunt. She appears to be extremely muscular and her hands are as large as those of a man, with powerful bony wrists and fingers. However, I have no wish for personal beauty in a housekeeper. Her other qualities are an ample compensation for her severe mien.

I thought I would test her to-day.

'What time was it when I came in?' I asked very casually when she was laying the table for my simple evening meal.

'Just five minutes to six,' she said sharply, without pausing to remember or consider at all.

What could be more precise or satisfactory?

'Thank you, Mrs Pluck,' I said. 'I'm afraid I'm a bit vague about time. You must keep me up to scratch, you know.'

'Your meals will always be ready on time,' she said rather

grimly and left me to sip the sweet sherry of which I have always been so fond.

Eighth Entry

I learnt something to-day which, if it is true, will mean that my decision in the matter of weapons has been made for me. A man called Richey, whom I have engaged to work in the garden two days a week, mentioned that the last tenant of 'Labour's End' had rented the shooting in Dead-man's Wood for an absurdly small price from the owner, who lives a dozen miles away.

'He only paid a pound or two for it,' Richey said. 'Be-cause there's nothing *there*. A few rabbits you might get and a left-over pheasant or two from the time they did pre-serve. But nothing to pay money for. Still if you *think* you could find any sport.'

I laughed inside myself. If I think I could find any sport. Richey would be surprised if he knew *what* sport I think I could find.

But it's an idea. If I do decide that a gun is the best weapon – well, there I am with a gun, and every right to be there. And if a man is found shot in Deadman's Wood it would have been an accident, or suicide, or somebody else. It could not possibly have been that little quiet studious man Mr Wellington Chickle. Why should it have been? What motive could he possibly have had?

I only wonder whether perhaps I'm getting away a little from my original conception – the spontaneous crime. I remember writing in this Journal that if a man of good character suddenly killed the *first person who came along*, unless he was actually seen in the act he could not be sus-pected. But am I beginning to complicate matters? I don't think so, really. I'm giving myself a reason for being in the place with the weapon *in case* I should be observed.

I am writing this evening to the owner of the shooting rights to see whether an arrangement can be made. If it can I think I'll decide on the gun. All details can wait for that.

Mrs Pluck gave me an excellent soufflé this evening. Really, that woman's a treasure. And when I enquired gently what time it was when I went to bed last night she answered me pat– Eleven-twenty, sir. I heard you close your door.' So even in the night hours she notices what time things happen.

Some new books arrived from Bumpus's to-day, or rather some old books they had been able to obtain for me. Among them some detective novels by a writer new to me – Leo Bruce. He relates the investigations of a certain Sergeant Beef, through an observer called Townsend. Very ingenious. But not as ingenious as I'm going to be. I should like to see Sergeant Beef at work on *my* crime!

CHAPTER FOUR

Journal of Wellington Chickle
Continued

Ninth Entry

I met Flipp and his wife to-day. Another piece of luck – Flipp is fond of shooting and goes down to the marshes, somewhere Rye way I gather, for duck when he can get petrol for his car. Hasn't done much since the war, but says he has a 12-bore. So that's three in the district – mine, Miss Shoulter's, and his. It begins to look as though the whole thing is being made too easy for me.

Flipp is a big man who is in some business in London which does not take too much of his time. He goes up to town twice or three times a week, I gather, and does not worry if he misses even that. If it is of any interest I can easily find out the nature of this business. He looks more like a farmer, a heavy hard-drinking man, who swears too much, even using rather strong language in the presence of his wife. She, poor woman, looks anaemic, a frost-bitten unhappy creature very much under Flipp's thumb.

I met them on the road on their side of the wood. I was taking a leisurely stroll and they came striding up behind me as though they were soldiers marching, at least Flipp walked like that and his wife hurried along beside him as though she was afraid of being left behind.

'You've just come to live at that bungalow with the silly name, haven't you?' was Flipp's greeting to me.

I showed no annoyance.

'Good afternoon,' I said, raising my hat. 'Yes, I have just come to live here. I suppose "Labour's End" does sound rather an odd name, but in my case it's appropriate, you know. My labours are ended, you see.'

'Lucky man,' said Flipp. 'How d'you like Barnford?'

'Charming. Charming,' I told him.

'Think so? Bloody awful hole, I think. Cold and damp.'

'I must say I haven't found it so,' I said.

'But you haven't spent a winter here yet, Mr Chickle,' his wife put in as though she had to say something.

'That's very true,' I smiled.

'Better come in and have a cup of tea,' said Flipp. 'Our place is just up the road.'

'I should be delighted. I wonder what made you come here if you think so little of the place?'

He did not seem to like that question and answered it rather gruffly.

'Edith Shoulter found the place for us.'

'Oh, you knew Miss Shoulter before you came here?' I asked. I was naturally interested.

'Known her for years,' grunted Flipp. 'That's our place you can see ahead of you.' And he began to take even longer strides so that I was quite out of breath when we arrived at 'Woodlands.'

The first thing I noticed in the hall was his gun — a 12-bore.

'Fond of shooting?' I asked casually.

It was then that he told me about the duck. I pretended to be only politely interested and soon changed the subject to gardening.

It was six o'clock when I got back to 'Labour's End', having refused a drink from Flipp before leaving. I found that the afternoon's post had come in and there was a letter from the owner of Deadman's Wood. He says that he cannot honestly ask anything but a nominal rent for the shooting since I shall find nothing but a few rabbits, but if I like to send him a fiver each season I am welcome to pot what I like over his ground. I chuckled at the phrase 'pot what I like.' He would be surprised if he knew its full implications for *me*.

Tenth Entry

It is past midsummer now, and a long time since I added anything to my Journal. The truth of the matter is I am in something of a quandary. My scheme seems to be losing its most essential quality, that of spontaneity. Willy-nilly I find myself making plans, just as lesser murderers must have done. I have to keep reminding myself that the secret of my success will lie in the casual nature of the enterprise. I still maintain that if I just go out and kill someone, anyone, without an elaborate design, I shall be safe from discovery; but that if I begin to play with strategy I shall call attention to myself. The trouble is that the ordinary precautions need so much forethought.

I remember when I was a boy at school we used to be given essays on set subjects–'Duty', 'A Day in the Country', and so on. A teacher told us one week to write an essay on any subject we liked. At first the very thought of this was thrilling. What scope! What a choice! But as we sat down to think it over, hesitating between one subject and another, each so attractive, we found it almost impossible to decide. I spent two days puzzling my head over it, and in the end did my essay on 'A Day in the Country' or 'Duty', or one of the old stock subjects, I forget which. It's like that now. I have a complete choice of time, place, method, and victim, and I find myself veering round inevitably to precedent, to planning my alibi and foreseeing police inquiries just as other murderers must have done.

However, other murderers had not the genius with which I approach the problem.

The gun for instance. Suppose I just shoot a stranger at that point on the path I have chosen. Well, it might have been Flipp with his gun, or anyone else with Flipp's gun, Miss Shoulter with her gun, or someone else with her gun, or someone using my gun, or someone altogether different with another gun. Nothing anyway to suggest that it could be me.

But another more interesting possibility occurs. Suppose the stranger, whoever he is, is found with a gun beside him from which both barrels have been fired, and suppose there are strings attached to the triggers and his fingerprints on the barrels, who could possibly suggest that it wasn't suicide? After all, I could make sure that I shot him from in front and at very close range – and that would conform perfectly. Everybody, for some queer reason, is more ready to believe in a man taking his own life than someone else's.

What about the gun, in that case? It mustn't be mine, that's certain. But it could very easily be either Miss Shoulter's or Flipp's. Both keep them very carelessly. With any luck I could come into possession of one or the other a week or so before the Great Day. The chances are that they would never even notice that the gun had gone, and if they did and reported it, well, I can always postpone the murder and start on a wholly different tack. It's all getting very interesting, and I scarcely ever need to read at night now. I just sit in the garden and dream of my triumph.

Eleventh Entry

Yes, that's how I'll do it. It's all clear now. A fortnight before the provisional date I'll get hold of either Miss Shoulter's or Flipp's 12-bore. This I will hide under the leaves in Deadman's Wood, wrapped up in an old piece of mackintosh I have. Then, on the appointed day, I will await my victim. If he comes, that is to say if anyone who is a stranger to me comes down the path, I will do it. If not, I will wait till another day, or another, till just the right person comes at just the right time. Then I will get him quite near me. I can think of many ways of doing that. I could pretend to have sprained my ankle and be flat on the ground waiting till he came close to me. Or I could show him something I was going to shoot and as he is looking let off the two barrels in his face. Half a dozen ways. Then get the other gun out of hiding and fix up the string as though he had shot himself.

Or maybe I might actually shoot him with the other gun. Why not? I should rather like to use my own trusty old 12-bore, but it would save an extra shot to use the other, because it would have to be fired off, anyway. I will consider the pros and cons of this. But anyway, that's the broad idea.

As soon as autumn comes I shall start going for a stroll

with my gun every evening towards dusk, and bringing home a rabbit or two. This must be known as my daily custom. I must let off a few shots, too, even if I don't see a rabbit so that people get used to the sound of a gun. And, of course, I shall have to take the normal precautions – footprints, fingerprints, and so on. Those will be child's play to me. And the question of time – I'll be careful of that. I shall have to make sure that a shot is fired after I've come in for the evening. At present I don't quite see how I'll do that, but I shall think of a way.

Twelfth Entry

September already. How this summer has flown. I think time does pass quickly, though, when one has some absorbing interest.

I've had a brilliant idea during the last few days. It is about the gun. I realized that a shot must be heard in the wood after I had returned to 'Labour's End' on the Great Day. How could I be sure of this? My idea is simple, but very effective. Suppose a gun were fixed to the branch of a tree a little way into the wood, and a ball of thin strong string passed round the trigger. All I would need to do would be to pull the string while I actually remained at 'Labour's End.' Complicated? Not a bit. The place for the gun would be about ten paces into the wood, far enough away for the report to come *from* the wood. I am quite sure Mrs Pluck could not gauge the actual distance. She would simply say she heard a shot in the wood. It must be in a straight line from the house – I don't want my string passing over anything. As for the string – its length inside the wood is no problem at all – I could 'lay' it on the night before the murder. The length of string across the lawn would be another matter. That afternoon I would be planning and laying out flower-beds and have a line running right across from my window to the wood, marking the edge of a path or a bed, or whatever you please. When it grew dusk I would tie this line to the double ends of the string already round the trigger of the gun. I would remain in the garden and look in at the window of the room to call Mrs Pluck. 'Oh, Mrs Pluck,' I would say, 'have you the right time? Half-past six? Thank you.' Then I would pull my line and away in the wood there would be a report. 'Someone shooting,' I would smile. 'They've no right to, but let it pass. A rabbit or two won't hurt us, will it, Mrs Pluck?' And later, when the body is found and it is believed that the man had been shot that afternoon — well, there's my alibi! Simple, isn't it?

Of course I shall remark to Mrs Pluck that I've stupidly left my line in the garden. 'Must bring it in,' I'll say. 'Someone might trip over it.' Always the considerate old gentleman, you see. Then I'll pop out and draw in the garden line and by drawing only one side of the double string pull in the other one from the gun. Then all I'll have to do is to go out that evening and get the gun or bring it back next day. Wait, though. *I* can choose *my* day. So it will be on Mrs Pluck's evening out, and when she has gone to the pictures over at Ashley — as she always does — I'll bring the gun in. Splendid. I'm beginning to enjoy this.

CHAPTER FIVE

Journal of Wellington Chickle
Continued

Thirteenth Entry

Another piece of luck has come my way, this time of a rather amusing kind. That pasty-faced curate came and asked me if I could manage to look in at the Jumble Sale at the Village Hall, and true to my benevolent character I agreed. There was the usual litter of rubbish – old books and clothes and ugly vases – and the usual crowd of tiresome people trying to find something on which they could spend a few shillings without wasting them.

There was a stall for old clothes over which the curate's sister, a plain and meaty girl who resembles her brother, was presiding. Right in front of her I saw a clothes-basket full of old boots and shoes, and on top of them a pair of the most enormous woman's walking shoes I have ever seen. They must have been size twelve at least, though there was a pretence of the feminine in their design. Under them was a pair of carpet slippers of my own size which I picked up and in which I pretended to take an interest.

'How much are these?' I asked, though my brain was already busy with a new idea suggested to me by the woman's shoes.

'Well, we were rather hoping to sell the whole basketful. As a lot, you know,' said the curate's sister.

Just what I hoped.

'Oh, dear!' I said good-humouredly. 'Whatever should I do with all these? How much would they be?'

'We hoped to get a sovereign, with the basket.'

'I think I could manage *that*,' I said, and gave her a pound note.

'It's very good of you,' grinned the curate's sister. 'All in a good cause, you know.'

Just as I was going away I picked up one of the woman's shoes.

'That's a big size,' I said. 'I wonder who wore those?'

The curate's sister seemed to enjoy the mild malice in her reply.

'Miss Shoulter,' she whispered. 'Huge feet. Haven't you noticed?'

'No, I haven't,' I said with just a suggestion of rebuke in my voice. 'I never notice that sort of thing.'

But my head was singing with excitement. Now I shan't even leave tracks on the Great Day. My feet will go into these easily and I'll keep them in the wood ready. On the afternoon I'll change into them for the task itself, then back into my own when it's over. The police, if they manage to find any footprints, will only know that Miss Shoulter has been near the scene of the crime.

So now I have defence in depth. The first line is suicide. The second Miss Shoulter. No one can even break through to my citadel. And there's always Flipp who has the same kind of gun.

Every day now I conscientiously take my walk in the afternoon with my gun. Now and again I get a rabbit and I've shot one pheasant already. I have met almost everybody in the course of these walks – Flipp and his wife, Miss Shoulter, the curate, the postman and a number of other people. Everyone knows that it's the custom of that nice old gentleman Mr Chickle to take a stroll with his gun in the afternoon. Just as it should be.

Fourteenth Entry

The chief problem now is that of getting hold of Miss Shoulter's gun. So easy, and yet a matter for great care. A slip over that would be disastrous – not for my safety but for the success of the present scheme.

She keeps it in the little front hall of her house. I consider that most reprehensible, really. A firearm is *not* a thing to leave lying about. But there it is, leant against the wall as though it were a walking-stick. All I have to do is to pick it up as I leave the house and walk away with it. No. one seeing me on my way back to 'Labour's End' would find anything odd in it – indeed, it would be the most normal thing since they would not dream that it was not *my* gun. And if by any chance Miss Shoulter herself should see me, or miss the gun so soon after my call that its disappearance would seem connected with me – then all I have to do is to plead absent-mindedness. 'How silly of me. I'm so accustomed to carrying a gun. Must have picked yours up by mistake.'

I shall have to become very friendly with Miss Shoulter, though. On 'popping-in' terms. I shall have to make her so accustomed to my visits that she won't even bother to see me out. That will be rather a bore. Her house is painfully untidy. She keeps no servant and her dining-room table nearly always has an opened tin on it. And she shouts so that conversation is trying. But she's a good-natured woman. It won't be difficult to establish the kind of relationship I need.

Of course, when I do take the gun, if anything goes wrong I postpone the whole scheme and then think of a new method altogether. No chances for me. But if she misses it a few days later and informs the police, all the better. *They* will have to discover after the murder how it came into the possession of the man who apparently shot himself with it. That's just the sort of thing that will suit the police. They'll work out some sort of theory to account for it, you may be sure.

Another thing I have to obtain in a way which will prevent its being connected with me is some kind of string, cord, tape, or ribbon with which to fake the suicide. You see how careful I am? Just that piece of cord could hang a man. And I've had a delightful idea about this, too. Red Tape! My victim shall be killed with red tape, just as it will be the red tape of the police force which will prevent his murderer being caught.

There's a lawyer in Ashley, and in a few days' time I will call on him and arrange a new will. I suppose I shall have to leave my money to my cousin's son, Rudolph Gooding. But I'll find a few improbable charities to endow with some of it. Gooding is such a prim conventional young man, engaged to an equally prim and colourless girl. He would never have the imagination to spend a large sum of money at all happily. But for the sake of form I will leave him the bulk.

Now while I'm in the solicitor's office I can surely find some red tape. I've often seen those little spools of it on lawyers' tables. If I don't see any lying about – well, it will just be too bad. I'll think of something else. As I assure myself again, *there's no hurry*. And red tape will add such a picturesque, such an ironic touch to my murder. Quite a treat for the crime reporters.

Fifteenth Entry

I think Christmas Eve would be a good time. Unless, of course, there is snow. I do *not* want a so-called white Christmas; it would show altogether too much of my movements. But if it's suitable weather, that would make a very good date, and another idea for the reporters.

All my preliminary preparations are made now, and we're still in November. Everyone is accustomed to seeing me with a gun and to hearing shots in Deadman's Wood. Miss Shoulter is so accustomed to my looking in on one pretext or another that she always leaves me to 'see myself out' as she calls it. (Actually, I think she thinks I'm in love with her, poor woman.) Flipp and his wife call on her nearly as often, and all three come to see me. The shoes are locked up in a trunk in my room. And Mrs Pluck can be relied on to notice any time at which anything happens, besides being accustomed to seeing me 'planning the garden' with a line on two pegs which I'm always moving about as I discuss new flower-beds and paths. In another week's time I can start really active measures.

Sixteenth Entry

I've got the gun! It was really too easy.

Of course, I took the greatest care. I did not leave my

home without a gun, you may be sure. I took my 12-bore, walked slowly away from 'Labour's End,' as I always do, and went to a spot in the wood I had already decided on. There I wrapped my gun in an old sheet of mackintosh and concealed it in the undergrowth. I walked on to Miss Shoulter's bungalow and found her very busy with a revolting new litter of pups. Also, she was concerned because her brother is expected this evening. I chatted for about ten minutes, then rose politely.

'I can see you're busy,' I said. 'So I won't waste your time. I do hope the puppies thrive. No, don't you move. You know I can see myself out.'

I left her kneeling on the floor with her dogs, carefully closed the door of her sitting-room and walked away as unconcernedly as you please with her gun under my arm. I did not meet a soul on my way to the place where my gun was hidden – not that it would have mattered if I had, for nobody could tell one gun from another. Then I unwrapped *my* gun, and wrapping hers, left it there. I was home at my usual time. It only remains to see how soon she misses it. Personally, I doubt if she will, until her attention is called to its absence by events. Those events! Not far away now.

Seventeenth Entry

And now I've got the red tape, too. I wonder why it's called red? It isn't red at all, but pink. However, I've got a dozen yards of it.

I called on Aston, the lawyer, by appointment yesterday. I found that he has only two rooms, his own and one where his solitary clerk sits, with two extra chairs for clients, I suppose. I sat in one of these waiting while Aston got rid of an imaginary visitor, and passed the time by chatting with the clerk. We earnestly discussed the weather and shortages of food and fuel. Then, touching some documents which were bound with the stuff, I asked whether that was what lawyers called red tape.

'Yes, indeed,' he said.

'But it's not red at all,' I ventured.

'No. Pink, isn't it?'

'Do you really use much of it?' I asked. 'Or is that just a joke in the comic papers?'

'We do use quite a bit,' he admitted.

'How is it sold to you?'

He pulled open a drawer and revealed a dozen or so spools of the stuff. He handed one to me to look at. I glanced at it but, seeming to lose interest, handed it back to him.

'I see,' I said indifferently. 'I should prefer paper-clips myself.' Then I went off into a long discussion on stationery.

But when the buzzer went and he hurried through to Aston's office my hand was in the drawer in a moment. And now I have a nice new spool of red tape.

After that the making of my will was almost pleasant. I've left sums of money to half a dozen obscure charities and £100 to Mrs Pluck if she's still in my service. The rest to Rudolph Gooding.

To-morrow will be December 20th. I am getting very excited as the day draws near. I went to see Miss Shoulter to-day for the first time since the afternoon on which I took the gun. Her brother had come and gone, she said, adding that she was sorry I hadn't met him. It appears that he is coming again for Christmas. About the gun she said nothing, though I gave her a lead by mentioning reported thefts in the district. I feel sure she does not know it has gone. How easy everything is made for me!

CHAPTER SIX

Journal of Wellington Chickle
Continued

Eighteenth Entry

To-day is Christmas Eve – the greatest day of my life, if all goes well. I intend to commit my murder at about four o'clock, or as soon after four o'clock as my victim comes walking down the footpath. Of course no one may come. That will be a pity, but it only means a postponement, for everything is ready. It is half-past two now, and I have a clear hour in which to make this, the most important entry in my Journal.

But first I must tell you about the cartridge. I remembered a few days ago that for the suicide a cartridge case (or two if the tape has pulled both barrels) must be found actually in the gun. You see how careful you have to be? A less intelligent murderer would have made a slip there and perhaps used a type of cartridge which was not found locally. So I asked Miss Shoulter where I could buy some cartridges.

'Don't think you'll get any now,' she said, 'unless you can persuade Warlock's to let you have some. They used to supply me and Flipp before the war.'

'What kind do they sell?' I asked.

'Potter's Fesantsure,' she said. 'At least that's what I always got, and Flipp the same.'

My own brand. Lucky again. So if I use these to fake the suicide, and the police decide that it wasn't suicide, there's still nothing to direct suspicion from Miss Shoulter or even Flipp.

Then fingerprints. Yesterday I went into the wood and polished every inch of Miss Shoulter's gun. To-day, of course, I shall wear gloves. No sense in taking any chances, even though I'm pretty sure it will pass as suicide. Whoever it turns out to be is sure to have something about him which

will provide reason enough for him to take his own life.
Who hasn't?

Also yesterday I went to my bedroom and took out the
pair of Miss Shoulter's shoes which I have kept locked up
there. I put them into the little haversack which I always
take with me when I take my evening stroll. I took them to
the place where the gun is hidden and put them beside it,
wrapped in a piece of old sacking. They'll be ready to-day.
And that was all before I went to bed last night, and slept
like a top. Everything, I felt, was in complete readiness. Not
a chance taken or a mistake made. I had nothing whatever
to worry about.

And now I will tell you how I have spent to-day, and you
will have a unique opportunity of seeing into the mind of a
murderer on the day of his crime. And a very unusual
murderer, too. One who not only will not be caught, but will
not even be suspected.

I had my early morning tea, then went to the window to
look at the weather. Excellent. It had rained in the night,
so that the ground will be nice and sticky to-day for footprints – of Miss Shoulter's shoes! – yet there is scarcely a
cloud visible now and everything promises a cold clear
day.

I came down to breakfast and found that Mrs Pluck had
managed to inveigle a kidney from the butcher. Delicious.
I *have* missed such things during the war. Kidneys, sheep's
hearts, liver, sweetbreads, brains – all the little etceteras of
meat which are so pleasing. I drank my coffee thoughtfully,
wondering what I should do first.

I decided that the most urgent matter was that of loading
my own gun and fixing it in the tree. I sent Mrs Pluck on
her bicycle to the village and while she was gone carried out
that simple operation. I found a branch about breast high
pointing away from the house, loaded the gun and tied it
firmly to the branch. Then I passed my long string round
the trigger and brought the double line back to my lawn,
seeing that from the foot of the tree to the edge of the lawn
it was hidden in the undergrowth. So now the ends were

ready for tying to the single thicker line I use for measuring out and marking flower-beds. All *that* was ready.

Then I went into the room where I keep my books, looked through my Journal from the beginning and went over in my mind exactly what I shall do this afternoon. After lunch I should work in the garden for a while, I decided, then at about half-past three I shall go for my stroll. Mrs Pluck usually has what she calls 'half an hour to herself' in the afternoon, disappearing into her little room on the east side of the house. From her window the front entrance is not visible so she will not be able to see that I go out without my gun. I shan't call her attention to the fact in case I am seen later with a gun under my arm. I will just walk slowly out as though it were an ordinary day.

Then I shall make my way to the place where the gun is hidden, unroll it from its mackintosh and load it. Then I shall take off my shoes and put on Miss Shoulter's. (I've already tried them, by the way. They are a little large, but I can easily walk in them.) Then I shall set off to the point, my point, where the fallen tree is. If I should happen to meet anyone on the way I feel quite convinced that he or she will not notice my shoes. But I shall keep my eye on him, watching *his* eyes. If I see him look down and I know that he has observed them, well, it will be all off till another time. But those are all ifs.

I suppose there is a slight danger, by the way, that I might meet someone who notices the shoes *after* the murder. It is very unlikely. And it is the only minute risk I am taking. After all, I can probably avoid anyone approaching – if anyone should be about.

To continue with my plan. I settle down behind my fallen tree trunk and wait. I am prepared to stay there for a full hour. And if a stranger comes it will be my great moment. I shall call him over. 'I'm afraid I've sprained my ankle,' I shall say. The gun will be beside me, leaning against the trunk in the most natural position. He will cross to see what is wrong. Then when he's quite near me, not more than a yard or so, he shall have both barrels in his face.

I shall then get busy. I shall first clean the outside of Miss Shoulter's gun which I shall be carrying, for although I shall have been wearing gloves all the afternoon it would be a useful extra precaution. Then I shall grip his fingers round it in a number of places. Then I shall tie the red tape to the triggers and set him as though he had been leaning over the gun while it was upright and had pulled the triggers with his foot. His foot will, in fact, be still in the loop which I shall tie in the tape. Right. He's there. An obvious suicide.

Slowly I shall walk away and back to the point where my own shoes are waiting. A quick change into these and I shall be ready for 'Labour's End'. 'Dear me, Mrs Pluck,' I shall say. 'I'm out late this evening.' 'It's only half-past five, sir,' she'll tell me. Then, I'll remember my gardening things including the line, and go out to get them in. It will be nice and dark by now so that I can tie my garden line to the double line round the trigger and let off the report in the woods without any trouble at all. Then all I have to do is to draw in my line and come in to enjoy my tea by a bright fire.

And there it will be – the perfect murder. Impossible of solution. And the victim? I do not know, and certainly do not care. It will be someone I have never seen before, that's all.

Later Mrs Pluck will come in to say that she's catching the Ashley bus and going to the pictures. 'Very well,' I shall say. 'You have your key?' And I shall be once again absorbed in my book. But when she has gone I shall go out quietly, untie my own gun, and bring it in. To-morrow, there will not be a single unusual thing about 'Labour's End'.

It leaves only one problem – Miss Shoulter's shoes. I don't want to keep them in my possession, and it would be better not to leave them in the wood, for one doesn't know how thoroughly the police will search it. They had best be cleared very soon, I think. If the body is found the same evening there will be no questioning or search for some hours. I think my best plan would be to put them in my haversack that night and run up to London for a day to-morrow. Then they could go out of the train window. Or would it be better to leave them where they are? The police would have to search twenty acres of woodland to find them. I think they would be safe there.

Next day will come what is called, I think, the hue and cry, and I shall know the name of my victim. It will not disturb me. 'Something attempted, something done', will certainly earn *me* a night's repose.

It is a quarter-past three now. The great moment is rapidly approaching. Mrs Pluck has just been in and I've given her her Christmas present. A touching scene – the benevolent old gentleman, the lonely housekeeper. She seemed grateful. And ironically enough there was the sound of a distant shot while we were speaking, so I needn't have bothered with my gun-in-the-tree idea at all. Still, I rather enjoyed that. It was so ingenious. I shall use it just the same.

And now I'm off. My great triumph is at hand. I only hope a suitable victim appears this afternoon. I am so excited that my hand is trembling and I can't write any more till afterwards.

CHAPTER SEVEN

Jack Ribbon Goes to Church

JACK RIBBON was sixteen years old and considered that his job as kennel-boy to Miss Shoulter was a good one. He was fond of dogs, fond of all animals for that matter, and in a desultory way was studying with the hope of one day becoming a veterinary surgeon. His hours of work were not too long and his pay was generous. He thought Miss Shoulter a bit of a gorgon, but he liked the straight way she talked to him, and used to say that it 'wasn't like working for a woman'.

Jack Ribbon was rather apt to talk of 'women' just then, for they had begun to interest him, and he them. He was considered the best dancer in Barnford and never missed one of the village hops. He was concerned with such matters as ties, brilliantine, and a new suit which he had just obtained from Ashley. He knew himself to be a presentable youth, fair-haired, light-skinned, quick of eye and movement, with an easy laugh which showed his excellent teeth. He found that he liked girls. A year ago he had not been aware of the fact. Now he was aware of little else.

Not that there was 'anyone special'. He knew all of them who came to the dances, but he had not yet started walking out with one. He was adept at the familiar slightly Americanized banter of the dance floor, but he had not yet started 'anything serious'.

He was not a remarkably inquisitive boy, but he could not help noticing things. Miss Shoulter's brother now – he did not like him. A sullen fellow who drank too much and 'treated the old girl rotten'. Jack could not make out why she put up with him. Yet every now and then he'd turn up at the bungalow, stay a night or two, drink anything he could lay hands on and, Jack believed, borrow a few quid from Miss Shoulter. He could not understand a woman who was so strong and downright in everything else being so weak over her brother, who, Jack thought, was nothing but a rotten sponger. He was supposed to make a living in some vague way out of horse-racing, but whether as a professional punter or a tout he would not like to say. Privately Jack did not believe that Shoulter had ever done a day's work in his life.

Last time he had been down there had been trouble – and it had something to do with Flipp. That was another thing Jack had never understood; what there was between Ron Shoulter and Flipp. Every time Shoulter came down he would go up to Flipp's place, usually in the evening, yet Flipp never came to Miss Shoulter's while her brother was there.

And last time, after her brother had gone, Jack Ribbon had seen an extraordinary thing. He had gone into the bungalow to see her about one of the dogs and had found the old girl in tears. He could scarcely believe it. Miss Shoulter, such a manly, noisy woman, sitting in an arm-chair crying her eyes out. He had not told anyone. It was the sort of thing Jack believed in keeping to himself. But it had made him think.

Then there was the old boy who had come to live at 'Labour's End'. He was pretty thick with Miss Shoulter now. In and out of the house every day. What was the idea? Decent old boy, mind you. He had given Jack ten bob as a Christmas present for no reason at all that he could see. And he was always smiling and spoke friendly. Still, you couldn't size him up. There was something funny about the old chap. And he did not like dogs.

Well, it was Christmas Eve. And to-morrow he'd be free all day except just for the feeding. But to-night he was going to Midnight Mass at the little church in Copling. His mother would not be able to come this year because of her rheumatism which had been chronic lately, though she'd never missed before. A good Catholic his mother, and she'd brought him up strict. She didn't mind him going to a dance and having a bit of fun, but let him miss Mass on

Sunday and see what would happen. Not that he wanted to miss Mass – particularly on Christmas Eve. The little church at Copling had been made out of an old barn and was still thatched. It was just like the real Christmas night, Jack thought.

So at eleven o'clock he started off from Barnford and began his lonely walk by the footpath through Deadman's Wood. Pity there was no one to go with him, but he and his mother were almost the only Catholics in the village, except for one family who would be going by car. Still he did not mind the walk and it was a nice clear night with lots of stars.

Jack Ribbon passed 'Labour's End' on the outskirts of the wood and noticed a light on in the housekeeper's room. She'd probably come back on the Ashley bus and was just turning in. The old man must have gone to bed – no light anywhere else in the house.

He followed the path by which old Chickle came when he called on Miss Shoulter. It was still a bit sticky underfoot from last night's rain, and you had to be careful how you walked.

Presently he reached a point in the path where there was a slight clearing and a fallen tree. It was here that old Chickle was always hanging about. He had heard Flipp tell Miss Shoulter that. 'The old boy's always standing about near that fallen tree beside the footpath,' Flipp had said. 'I wonder what the idea is?' Miss Shoulter had laughed and said that he was probably waiting for rabbits to come out. But Flipp had seemed very puzzled. 'I've met him half a dozen times, and always in the same spot.'

Jack was early for Mass. The church was only ten minutes away now and it was not yet half-past eleven. He crossed to the fallen tree, sat down on it and lit a cigarette.

When he told the story afterwards he could not say exactly what had made him look on the ground behind him. He did mutter something incoherent about feeling as though someone was watching him, but admits that was just his imagination. But look he did, then jumped to his feet. The first thing he saw was the dirty old teddy-bear overcoat which Ron Shoulter always wore. Perhaps it was this which made him certain that the Thing behind him was, or had been, Ron Shoulter. He never had any doubt of it at the time or afterwards, though it was not by the face that he recognized it, for the very sufficient reason, which he gave between chattering teeth later, that there wasn't any face. In fact what he saw was a corpse with – as he put it – the best part of its head blown off.

He did not, he could not, touch it. He thinks he gave some sort of a shout. Then he set off as fast as he could and did not stop running till he came out of the wood. He was very scared.

The first thing he wanted to do was to get among people. Talk to someone. As he came to 'Labour's End' he saw that the light was still on in the housekeeper's room and without thinking very clearly he hurried up to the front door and gave the electric bell a long ring. As he waited he watched the footpath into the wood as though he thought someone might be following him.

Mrs Pluck came to the door.

'What ... Why, Ribbon, what on earth ...' she began.

'A dead man,' he said. 'A dead man in the wood.'

A light showed in another window and in a few moments Mr Chickle came to the door in a thick woollen dressing-gown.

'What's this?' he asked rather snappily. 'Young Ribbon, what do you want at this time?'

'I ... just found a dead man, sir. In the wood. Just near that place where you often go. ...'

Mr Chickle seemed cross.

'Place where *I* often go?' he repeated frowning.

'Yes, sir. You know, by the fallen tree. He's dead. Half his head blown off. I think it's Miss Shoulter's brother.'

If Mr Chickle had seemed angry before he was much more so now.

'Miss Shoulter's brother! What makes you think that, young man?'

'It's got his coat on,' said Jack Ribbon lamely.

Mr Chickle seemed to have recovered himself.

'Well, really, Ribbon, I don't see why you should come and wake *us* up at this time of night. I was asleep and I expect Mrs Pluck was just going to bed. If as you say you've found some evidence of an accident, surely you should know that it's your duty to report it to the police. Not to come ringing our door-bell.'

'Yes, sir. I was a bit upset....'

Then Mr Chickle became more like his old self.

'I must say you look upset, Ribbon. I'm sure it was very distressing. And since you *are* here and Mrs Pluck has not retired, you'd better drink something before you go to find the police. Give him a drop of brandy, Mrs Pluck.'

'Thank you, sir. I didn't ought to wait really. I ought to tell the police. It was a horrid sight, really it was. No head to speak of left, you might say.'

Mrs Pluck brought some brandy in a medicine glass, as though she wanted to stress the fact that it was restorative and not festive. Jack swallowed it.

Mr Chickle did not seem at all interested in the 'horrid sight'. He asked no questions at all, and when the brandy was finished told Jack to hurry down to the village.

'I expect you'll find Constable Watts-Dunton in bed,' he said. 'But you should knock him up in view of what you have found. Please tell him not to disturb me again to-night, however. He will know what arrangements to make.'

Jack, feeling a little better, hurried on to the village and knocked at the constable's door. It was ten minutes before he got any answer and then a woman's head appeared at an upper window.

'Yes?' said Mrs Watts-Dunton.

'Tell the constable there's a dead man in Deadman's Wood,' said Jack breathlessly.

'I'll tell the constable,' suddenly shouted his wife. 'And you'll see what happens to you, young Ribbon. He knows all about you and your silly larks. Now you've gone a bit too far, let me tell you. Waking people up ...'

Jack began to lose his temper.

'It's true, I tell you. I've seen him myself. Half his head blown off.'

'What d'you mean?'

'You call the constable. There's nothing funny about this. If you'd seen what I've seen.'

The window was closed, but after ten minutes Constable Watts-Dunton himself appeared at the door, fully clothed.

'What's this?' he asked severely, as though Jack Ribbon was certainly to blame for something or other.

'It's what I say. A dead man in Deadman's Wood.'

Constable Watts-Dunton, a thin and very solemn man who attended a chapel called Mount Sion and disapproved of most human activities, suddenly leant forward to sniff at Jack Ribbon's breath.

'Have you been drinking?' he asked in a hollow voice.

'I had a tot of brandy from Mr Chickle,' admitted Jack. 'I was upset, see? It's not a nice thing to happen to anybody.'

'What isn't?' asked Constable Watts-Dunton.

'Finding a stiff in a wood with its head blown off.'

'And what were you doing in the wood at this time?' asked the constable.

'On my way to church. Midnight Mass at Copling.'

'No wonder,' said Constable Watts-Dunton darkly, but did not enlarge on this cryptic negative.

'I believe it's Ron Shoulter,' added Jack.

'Oh, you do? Well, we'll have to look into all that. You'd better come along and show me where you found whatever you have found. Wait a minute while I get my torch.'

So the police began their investigations rather earlier than Mr Chickle had anticipated.

CHAPTER EIGHT

It was Murder

WHEN Sergeant Beef and I arrived in Barnford it was New Year's Eve, and the first rush of local excitement over the body found in Deadman's Wood was beginning to subside.

We alighted at the station at about midday and Beef at once turned his mind to the question of our quarters. I have noticed on previous occasions that until he is what he calls 'fixed up' Beef will not begin to take any part in the investigations in hand.

'Which is the best pub?' he asked the ticket-collector.

'Depends what for,' the man said slowly. 'The beer's best at the Feathers, but there's some nice people keeping the Crown. I should say the Feathers' darts was better, but if you want a good warm fire in the bar the Crown's the place. When it comes to company . . .'

At last Beef cut this short.

'I want to put up for a few nights,' he said.

'Then you better try the Crown. The Feathers don't do anything of that.'

'How do I get there?'

'Follow this road till you come to Potter's the butchers, then turn right. It's on your left.'

'Thanks,' said Beef, and picking up his suitcase marched off.

'May as well be comfortable,' he explained. 'A nice little case like this should be enjoyable if we get decent quarters.'

I made no comment, though I could have pointed out the discrepancy between a corpse in a wood and 'enjoyment'.

We found the Crown and Beef made for the Public Bar. Not until the beer in his pint glass had sunk by three or four inches did he approach the object for which we had presumably come to the inn.

'Do you go in for accommodation?' he asked the plump, middle-aged woman who had served us.

'That depends,' she said with a guarded look at Beef's red face.

'I was wanting to put up for a few days,' explained Beef.

'Commercial?' asked the landlady.

'Certainly not. I'm here to investigate the violent death of Mr Ronald Shoulter.'

He spoke in his most impressive accents. I could have kicked him for giving away our business.

'Scotland Yard?' asked the landlady with some animation. Beef shook his head.

'Private,' he explained. 'Representing the sister of the deceased. This gentleman' – for the first time I was included in Beef's negotiations – 'is Mr Townsend, who writes up my cases.'

'Well!' said the landlady.

'We could do with a couple of rooms,' Beef continued.

I did not blame the landlady for hesitating. Beef being solemn and important was not an imposing sight.

'I don't think we should give you much trouble,' I intervened with a smile.

The landlady still seemed dubious.

'I'll ask my husband,' she said at last, and disappeared through a door behind the bar.

A few minutes later a little quick-spoken grey-haired sparrow of a man hurried in.

'Bristling's my name,' he said. 'Pleased to meet you. Detectives, eh?'

Beef cleared his throat.

'Private investigators,' he said.

'On this job in Deadman's Wood, I hear. Think it was murder?'

'I have not yet commenced inquiries.' said Beef loftily.

'I see. Well, I don't see why we shouldn't put you up. Staying long?'

'Difficult to say,' said Beef. 'Ve-ry difficult to say.'

'Well, we'll do what we can. Mother! Show them the rooms.'

'I think we'll have the other half first,' said Beef. 'What about you?'

When our glasses were refilled and Mr Bristling had his, Beef clumsily led the conversation to the matter in hand.

'What's thought about it in the village?' he asked.

'Well, we know the party. The dead party, I mean. As a matter of fact I had to ask him to leave here one night. Caused trouble.'

'What sort of trouble?'

'Argument, leading to threats. He was fond of his liquor, see, and didn't know when to stop. And when he'd had a few he got nasty. Very nasty, sometimes. That particular night he was arguing with Joe Bridge, a young farmer from Copling way.'

I became interested at once. With any luck this Bridge would be a suspect. I feel that in order to make Beef's investigations interesting to the reader it is as well to have as many suspects as possible.

'Has he a gun?' I asked.

I could see that Beef did not like my quick-witted entry into the conversation. And I don't think that Mr Bristling did, either.

'Yes, Joe's got a gun. What farmer hasn't?'

'You was telling us about Shoulter,' said Beef.

'Yes, he was a nuisance. Whenever he came down to stay with his sister he'd be round here or the Feathers drinking himself silly and quarrelsome. Owes me a bit of money, too.'

'Think anyone had a grudge against him? A real grudge, I mean.'

'Nobody liked him. But that's not to say anyone 'ud blow his brains out. Course, he was in with the people who live up in the wood – Flipps. That's another one who likes his liquor. But he has it at home. Sends down for bottles when he can get them, and seems to get a bit from London. What there was between him and the Shoulters I don't know.'

'Ah!' said Beef.

'Tell you what,' said Mr Bristling. 'There's young Jack Ribbon who works for Miss Shoulter. He'll know more. It was him found the body, too.'

Out came Beef's enormous note-book, a relic of his days in the Force, and I saw him write in his laborious hand 'J. Ribbon' and underneath it, 'J. Bridge'.

'Then there's the old gent that came to live here about a year ago. He might have heard something. Lives on the outside of the wood. Chickle, his name is.'

'Initial?'

'W.'

'Thanks. That's a start anyway.'

'Inquest's to-morrow.'

'Been a long time over it, haven't they?'

'It's been put off, I understand.'

'Who's in charge of the police investigation?'

'An inspector from Ashley. Name of Chatto.'

'Well, you've been very helpful.'

Mr Bristling had not finished yet.

'There's the constable here, of course. *He's* not much use, except for hanging round at closing time. Proper spoil-sport he is. Chapel.'

'What's his name?'

'Watts-Dunton.'

'What?'

'Watts-Dunton. With a hyphen.'

'Gor'!' said Beef. 'I don't know what the Force is coming to since I left it. Constables with hyphens. I once had a young constable called Galsworthy under me, and that was bad enough.'

'There you are,' said Mr Bristling. 'And he's a misery. Now what about lunch for you gents? I'm afraid there's nothing much *in*. Still, we'll see what the missus can do.'

It was not until nearly three o'clock that we left the Crown, and I was getting impatient.

'No sense in hurrying,' said Beef. 'I've got to think.'

'Whom do we see first?' I asked.

'We'll do things correct,' said Beef. 'And call at the Police Station.'

This turned out to be the semi-detached house in which Constable Watts-Dunton lived. It was marked by a blue plate and a blue lamp. Beef marched up to the door and knocked boldly.

My first view of Constable Watts-Dunton confirmed the description given by Mr Bristling. He was a tall, cadaverous man who would have been in his element with a banner warning us that the Day of Judgement is at hand.

'Well?' he asked.

'I should like to see the inspector in charge of the Shoulter Case,' said Beef.

'Have you got any information for him?' asked the constable with a mixture of gloom and self-importance.

'Not yet. You tell him Sergeant Beef would like to see him.'

Watts-Dunton disappeared and returned to say that Inspector Chatto would spare him five minutes. We were shown into a little room in which there was a bright fire. At the table Inspector Chatto sat before a stack of papers. He was stout, clean-shaven, rather jovial, but I saw that he had quick, shrewd eyes.

'You've heard of me?' asked Beef rather anxiously.

''Fraid not,' said the inspector genially.

Beef turned on me almost savagely.

'There you are!' he said. 'Never heard of me. What did I tell you?' Then, turning again to Inspector Chatto, he said: 'Now if I was Lord Simon Plimsoll or Monsieur Amer Picon, or Mr Albert Campion, or one of them, you'd know of me quick enough, wouldn't you?'

'I'm not a great reader,' said Inspector Chatto. 'But I do know of these. Private detectives in novels, aren't they?'

'That's right,' said Beef. 'And that's what I am, or what I ought to be if Mr Townsend here was as good at his job as I am at mine. Five cases I've handled, inspector, and got the answer every time, though Inspector Stute himself will tell you ...'

'I know him, of course.'

I saw that it was time to interrupt.

'Inspector,' I said firmly, 'my friend here talks a little impulsively at times. But what he says is substantially true. He is, in fact, a very clever investigator, and Inspector Stute will acknowledge his indebtedness to Beef on more than one occasion. I do trust you won't be put off by my friend's rather rough appearance and manner. I feel sure he can be of assistance to you. He is retained in this case by Miss Shoulter.'

Inspector Chatto lit a cigarette. He seemed rather amused.

'I have no wish at all to discourage amateurs,' he said. 'And I'm quite prepared to believe that Sergeant Beef may be of assistance to us. But what exactly do you mean when you say that he is "retained" by Miss Shoulter?'

This was awkward. Beef had the sense to keep quiet and leave it to me.

'Er – Miss Shoulter is under the impression that the police believe her brother's death to be suicide. She is convinced that it is nothing of the sort. She wishes Sergeant Beef to collect any evidence there may be to that effect.'

Inspector Chatto was smiling openly now.

'And if I tell you that the police are convinced of the same thing?'

'You mean?'

'I mean it was murder.'

There was an awkward silence.

'In that case the only honourable thing for Sergeant Beef to do will be to tell Miss Shoulter that since the police are now convinced, there is no need for her to employ him.'

Inspector Chatto looked at both of us.

'You were expecting to get a book out of this, Mr, er –'

'Townsend. Yes, I did rather hope –'

'Exactly. Well, frankly I see no reason for the two of you to leave. It *is* an interesting little case. And at present I'll tell you frankly we haven't much in the way of a clue. Since you've come down here you may as well wait for the inquest.'

'That's very friendly of you, inspector.'

Beef nodded towards the stack of papers.

'What about telling me what you've got?' he asked crudely.

Inspector Chatto chuckled.

'I see no objection,' he said. 'I should rather like to go over the case from the beginning. It might clear my ideas a bit. Watts-Dunton, d'you think your good lady could manage a cup of tea for us?'

Watts-Dunton's face came as near to producing a smile as its gaunt features would allow it.

'She's got the kettle on now,' he said.

'Then let's get down to it,' said Chatto.

So in this amiable atmosphere, which Beef really owed to my ready apology for him and my explanation of his abilities, we were taken into the confidence of the police.

CHAPTER NINE

Police Confidences

'WHAT you want to know, of course,' began Inspector Chatto, 'is what makes us think it was murder. That's simple enough. The corpse was found with a length of red tape round his foot which was attached to the trigger of the gun. The inference being that he held the gun in an upright position, leaned over it and fired it with his foot. His head in that case could not have been more than eighteen inches at the most away from the gun. Now, if you care to read the medical evidence and the report of the ballistics expert you will find that in point of fact the gun was at least four yards, possibly more, from Shoulter when it was fired.'

Beef nodded knowingly.

'That makes it murder,' he said. 'That's good. I do hate suicide. Nasty panicky little crime. What else did the experts have to say?'

'Not a great deal. The doctor did not see the body until early on Christmas morning. He could not say more than that the man had been dead for anything from nine to sixteen hours, that is to say that Shoulter was killed between one p.m. and eight o'clock on Christmas Eve.'

'Not very helpful.'

'The bullet man was better. You can be pretty accurate when it's a shot-gun. The spread of the shot and so on. He believes that Shoulter was coming up the path, that is to say walking from Barnford towards Copling. That would be his quickest way from Barnford to his sister's bungalow. The man who shot him was hidden on the wood side of a little clearing beside the path. You can see the place. There's a fallen tree there which would make excellent cover. When Shoulter was about level with the murderer he probably looked towards him, because he got both barrels in his face. His distance in that case would be just four yards. Then the murderer must have rigged the thing to look like suicide. He had some red tape in his pocket and tied it round the barrel and made a loop for the man's foot. Then he dragged the corpse across the clearing and dumped it behind the tree. There was evidence of the body being dragged across the wet, sticky ground.'

'Did you see that yourself?' asked Beef.

'Yes. Constable Watts-Dunton here had the sense to get me out at once, though it *was* Christmas Day. When I came to have a look at the place I found everything untouched since the crime, except just for the footprints of young Jack Ribbon who found the body at eleven-thirty on Christmas Eve. It was very useful. There was no doubt about the body having been dragged across the clearing, though very determined efforts had been made to destroy the marks of dragging.'

'Footprints, you said,' prompted Beef.

'Yes. They were interesting. There were the dead man's coming from Barnford and stopping short on the footpath about half-way across the clearing. There were Jack Ribbon's coming from Barnford and turning off to go to the tree on which he sat down for a smoke that night before he found the corpse. And the only other ones were – guess!'

'Joe Bridge's,' I said at once, remembering how astutely I had already secured his name as a suspect.

Chatto positively goggled at me.

'What makes you say that?' he asked.

'Never mind Mr Townsend,' said Beef rudely. 'He'd say anything.'

'I'm interested,' the inspector told him. 'We *have* heard about this young Joe Bridge. Had a row with Shoulter, didn't he? Know any more?'

I had to admit that at present I did not know any more.

'Well, there were some of Bridge's. But it looked as though he had simply walked down the path from Copling. There were some more interesting ones than that. The footprints we particularly noticed were those of Miss Shoulter.

the dead man's sister. And your client,' he added with a rather malicious smile.

'Were they new?' said Beef. 'When had it rained last?'

'Night of the twenty-third – twenty-fourth,' said Chatto. 'These had all been made on Christmas Eve. Of course,' he conceded as though he wanted to be kind. 'Of course the clearing could have been approached by other ways which would have left no footprints at all. You could come up between the trees and if you were careful and avoided patches of mud you wouldn't need to leave a mark.'

'I see. Now what about this Shoulter?'

'The dope on him is coming in every day. Masses of it. No good at all. Goes in for professional punting and has been mixed up with some pretty shady lots on the race-course. Started as a chemist. Was bookie's clerk for a time. A drunk and a sponger. He was a parents' darling as a child and when the old people died went rotten. Ran through what they left him and did his best to get the little bit left to his sister. One report says that he's not above blackmail. No loss, and anybody's victim.'

'How long had he been in Barnford?'

'Arrived that morning from London on a train that gets in at two-fifty. Too late for a drink, but went to the back door of the Feathers and asked the landlord, a man named Brown, if he could have one. Brown says he refused and that Shoulter walked off at once. But of course we can't be sure about that. He may have sat there drinking all the after-noon. We only know for certain that he came off the train at two-fifty. No one except Brown admits to having seen him alive again.'

'I see,' said Beef. 'That's all very clear and interesting.'

'There's a lot more stuff,' said Chatto.

'Yes. I was just going to ask about the gun.'

'Your client's again,' smiled Chatto. 'But she did report to the police about seven days before the crime that she had lost it. Taken from her front hall. Says she had no idea when it went. The last time she had seen it to her know-ledge was when her brother had been down a month ago.

He had taken it out one afternoon to try and get a rabbit. She can't be sure that he put it back in its usual place in the hall. She only knows that about a week before Christmas she noticed that it wasn't there. She asked young Ribbon and he said that he hadn't seen it for some days. The last time he positively remembers seeing it was when she told him to clean it once in October. He put it back after that.'

'What about cartridges?'

'Potter's Fesantsure were in the gun,' said Chatto. 'The local firm, Warlock's of Ashley, say that they supplied these to most of the people round here who had licences. That includes Miss Shoulter, a man named Flipp who lives in the wood, a retired watchmaker named Chickle who lives at a bungalow called 'Labour's End' at the Barnford end of the footpath through the wood, a solicitor named Aston with an office in Ashley and a bungalow at Copling, and your friend Joe Bridge.'

'Any interesting fingerprints?'

'None. The gun had been wiped dry and then gripped by the dead man, presumably after death by someone holding his hand round the barrel. None on anything else that we've found. Gloves, of course.'

'Any idea when the shots were fired?'

'Pretty contradictory. Both Flipp and a woman named Mrs Pluck who is housekeeper to Chickle, whose first name, by the way, is Wellington –'

'Wellington?' shouted Beef.

'Wellington. After the Iron Duke.'

'Blimey, you haven't half got some names round here.' And he gave a rude stare at Watts-Dunton.

'I was saying that Mrs Pluck, Flipp, Chickle himself and Miss Shoulter say they heard a double shot at about twenty past three. Mrs Pluck, Miss Shoulter, and Flipp heard the same thing about an hour later, but Chickle says that was himself potting at a hare. Then Chickle and Mrs Pluck, but not Miss Shoulter or Flipp, heard another shot, which might have been two barrels fired simultaneously, at exactly six-five. They're sure about the time as Chickle was putting away his gardening things just then and called Mrs Pluck's attention to the fact that someone was poaching.'

Mm. Now what I'd like to know is this. Suppose Shoulter was shot with the gun he was holding, is there anything to make us certain of that? Could he have been shot with one gun, then this one discharged and put by him by the murderer?'

'He could. Nothing to prevent it. But no reason to think so. Why should the murderer use two guns?'

'I was wondering perhaps whether Shoulter borrowed his sister's gun last time he was down and had it with him that afternoon. She can't swear to seeing it since he was in the house before. The murder might have been done with another gun, then this one fired off in the air and used to fake the suicide.'

'Conceivable,' agreed Chatto. 'And it had occurred to me. There's nothing final against it, but two reasons why I don't think it's likely. First the ticket-collector remembers seeing Shoulter when he got off the train but does not remember his having a gun. He says he believes he had a golf bag, so I admit it could have been in that, but it doesn't seem very likely. However, I still have an open mind. The second reason is that none of the double reports heard came near enough to one another. I mean, if he was going to fake it to look like suicide he – or she – would surely attend to that at once. There was nearly an hour between the first double report and the second, and an hour and a half between the second and third.'

'Of course,' said Beef slowly. 'If it was premeditated, and someone knew Shoulter would be coming off that train and walking up to his sister's house, he could have fired the barrels of Miss Shoulter's gun the day before in readiness.'

'True – though there are a lot of ifs. And *why* would he do that? Why not use the gun first for the murder, then leave it there for the faked suicide?'

'No reason. I was just looking all round, if you know what I mean. How about alibis?'

'Well, we haven't touched on that much, as we haven't got

a suspect yet. Of the people who lived round about, for what they're worth, very few have an alibi for much of the time, and none for all of the time. Miss Shoulter went out on her bicycle at about four and says she went to Copling (which you can reach by road from her place). She went to post a letter and can't remember whom she may have met, if anyone. Joe Bridge was with his cowman till about five, then drove off in his car. He was in the Crown soon after opening-time, which is six o'clock around here. Aston, the solicitor –'

'Why have you got *him* in?' asked Beef.

'Well, he has a gun, some Fesantsure cartridges, and he *is* a solicitor.'

'But that doesn't make him a murderer, surely? Though I dare say there's many a solicitor must *feel* like murder with the silly things people come to them with.'

'No. But it does mean that he might have had red tape in his pocket,' said Chatto, and left this to sink in.

'Yes,' said Beef after a moment. 'And who else?'

'Little Mr Chickle left his house at three-thirty, and was back at ten to five. His housekeeper's a sort of walking alarm clock, and notices all his times of coming and going. Then Mrs Pluck went off to the pictures in Ashley at six-thirty and young Jack Ribbon finished work at four. Flipp has no one to testify to his movements at all. His wife's away and he'd let their servants, two sisters from Ashley, go home for Christmas. Says it was his only chance of keeping them for another month or two. He says he was indoors all day. Never left his house at all. Of course you understand these are not our suspects. They're really the only people whose movements could seem of the least possible interest. You may find some more whom we've not yet come on.'

'Who *are* your suspects?' asked Beef.

Chatto hesitated.

'Frankly,' he said at last, 'we haven't any. Of course, Miss Shoulter's footprints *do* take some explaining, and she's not helpful. She says that she never used the footpath that day. The only time she went out was on her cycle. Quite positive about it, she is. A very downright woman. But I don't suspect her. I cannot see what possible motive she could have had. Shoulter had no money. And she appears to have been quite fond of the wretched man.'

'Then the police,' I put in with a disarming smile, 'are what the newspapers called baffled?'

'That's about it,' said Chatto complacently. 'But I think we shall get at something from the other end, as it were. When we've learnt all there is to learn about the dead man we shall know that *someone* here had a motive. We shall start from there. Motive's the thing, every time. You can't go wrong if you find the motive.'

'I suppose you're right,' said Beef. 'Only sometimes there's a lot of motives, and a lot of people with them.'

'Yes, there is *that*,' admitted Chatto.

Beef stood up.

'Very grateful to you,' he said. 'And now I suppose I get to work. But I've got no big ideas, inspector. In fact I've got only one idea at present, and it's this. I think we're going to find this case a lot more difficult and a lot more interesting than it looks. Anyway, I'll come and see you again. And if I should hit on anything I shan't forget that you've let me in on this.'

Inspector Chatto gave us his ready little smile again. But my ears burned when I thought what he must be saying to Constable Watts-Dunton about Beef when we had left the house.

Beef disgusted me further by turning back to the Crown.

'Quite enough for to-day,' he said. 'I want to think. Besides, it's opening time.'

CHAPTER TEN

Flipp was not at Home

But Beef was up and busy early next morning as is his infuriating habit. He will let everything wait overnight while he plays his eternal darts and drinks his beer, then expect me to start the day's work with all the cheerfulness and enthusiasm of a young boy.

'Come on,' he said, while I was still sitting at the breakfast table. 'We've got to go and see Miss Shoulter.'

I rose unwillingly and we started off for Deadman's Wood. We had learnt from willing informants in the bar on the previous evening, informants whom Beef had tried to impress with talk of 'private investigations', that we could reach her bungalow by the fatal footpath, passing first 'Labour's End', the home of the retired watchmaker with the absurd name, and then the spot where the crime had actually been committed.

On our way through the village we met Inspector Chatto who gave us a friendly greeting.

'On the job, eh?'

'Ah,' said Beef. 'There was one point I wanted to ask you about. Those footprints. You said they were Miss Shoulter's. What made you so sure? Was there something special about them which corresponded to a pair of her shoes?'

Chatto laughed outright.

'Wait till you see her feet!' he said. 'Couldn't mistake 'em. I doubt if there's another woman in the county who takes that size.'

'Large, are they?'

'Large? You've never seen such plates of meat in your life. The footprints were hers, all right. Rubber soles which she always wears, I understand, and an outsize. But women's shoes with semi-high heels."

'I've got you,' said Beef, and we walked on.

We passed 'Labour's End' and noticed an old gentleman at work in his garden.

'That must be Wellington Chickle,' I whispered.

'We'll see him later,' promised Beef. 'It's Miss Shoulter I want to talk to now.'

We were stopped again by our arrival at what Beef called 'the Spot'. It was a pleasant place. It seemed a pity that it should have been defiled by a brutal crime. It was a clearing about twelve or fifteen yards wide, and the path ran right across it. To our left as we walked was a fallen tree, about six yards back from the path on the verge of the wood itself. It was behind this that the corpse had been found.

There was nothing to see here now, as Beef himself admitted, for it was nearly a week since the murder, and dozens of people had tramped about since then. There were some scratches about six feet from the ground in the bark of a tree to our right which had been marked with chalk, and Beef decided these had been caused originally by shot and examined by experts.

'They can tell the distance from them,' he remarked. And when he had gazed long at the wood about us he added that anyone could have approached the spot without using the path, and left no footprints at all.

We stood there in silence for a long time, and I wondered whether Beef was expecting a flash of inspiration to descend on him and reveal the murderer's identity. I asked him as much.

'No. Just thinking,' he said, and we walked on.

Miss Shoulter greeted us from her kennels in her ringing voice.

'Hullo!' she shouted, and when she had joined us at the gate, added, 'I'm glad you've come. The damn fools think it's me now.'

Beef took this very seriously.

'Inspector Chatto's no fool,' he said. 'And what makes you think he suspects you?'

'Tell it a mile off,' said Miss Shoulter, slapping her jodhpurs with a stick. 'Keeps asking me what I was doing in the wood that day. Never went near the place.'

'Do you think there is somewhere we could go to talk a little more discreetly?' I asked, hoping she might take the hint and lower her voice.

'Not a soul here except Ribbon and *he*'s all right. My kennel-boy, you know. Came on the body on his way to church.'

'Yes, but others might be within earshot,' I said, lowering my own voice as an example to her. I was thinking privately that earshot was a wide term when it referred to Miss Shoulter's vocal powers.

'Come in then,' she invited. 'No one in the house. Haven't got any servants.'

'Expensive, aren't they?' suggested Beef.

'It's not that so much. Between you and me I could have afforded a good many things I did without. It was that brother of mine. I had to pretend to be broke or he'd have had it out of me. He couldn't keep money, poor chap....'

'We'll come to that in a minute,' said Beef. 'There's something I've got to tell you first. I understand that you engaged me because the police thought your brother's death was suicide and you wanted this disproved. Well, I am breaking no confidence when I tell you that the police are now convinced that it was not suicide, and that at the inquest to-day there will probably be a verdict of murder against some person or persons unknown. So perhaps you'll no longer require my services.'

'Good Lord, yes,' said Miss Shoulter. 'I tell you the fools think I did it. I don't want to face a murder charge. You'd better keep going and find out who did do it.'

Beef coughed.

'In that case you understand that what I shall be looking for is the truth. I could not undertake a case with any special axe to grind.'

Miss Shoulter laughed.

'That's all blah,' she said. 'I've read that stuff in detective novels. You know perfectly well I didn't do it.'

'You'll forgive my pointing out that we know nothing of the sort,' I put in. 'Of course we don't *think* you did it. But what Sergeant Beef wants to say is that he will bring to book *whoever* murdered your brother.'

'That's all right,' said Miss Shoulter. 'Now ask what questions you like.'

'There are rather a lot, I'm afraid,' said Beef. 'First of all about the footprints –'

'Footprints?'

'Perhaps I oughtn't to have mentioned that. But the police found footprints near the place where the body was found which corresponded to your own.'

Miss Shoulter stared.

'Must have been old ones,' she said.

'It rained the night before.'

'Can't have been mine then. Yet I should have thought my feet were pretty unmistakable. I have to have my shoes made specially."

'Exactly,' I murmured.

'But I didn't go down the wretched path. Dammit, I'd tell you if I did.'

Beef spoke slowly.

'In that case there's only one possible explanation and it makes this crime look uglier than ever. Have you ever missed a pair of shoes?'

'No. Can't say I have.'

'Perhaps you'd just go and check on what you've got.'

'That's easy. I've only got three pairs.'

She left us.

'Do you think she's lying?'

'No,' said Beef. 'She's speaking the truth.'

She was soon back.

'None missing,' she said.

'Think back carefully, now. Over the last year, say.'

'Tell you what,' she said at last. 'I sent a pair to the Jumble Sale a few months ago. Pretty well done for, they were. I wondered who could possibly want them.'

'They were sold?'

'I suppose so. You'd better see Eva Packham about that. She had the old clothes stall. She's the curate's sister.'

'I will,' said Beef, and made one of his laborious notes.

'Do you think that someone *wore* them — to incriminate me?' asked Miss Shoulter.

'We shall see,' said Beef severely. 'Now about this brother of yours.'

Her breezy manner dropped for a moment. I was watching her closely, and I could understand what Chatto had meant when he said that he believed she was quite fond of the wretched man.

'He was what you call a bad hat,' she said. 'No doubt of that. Mother and Father spoilt him as a child. And I've never been able to do much with him. He was two years older than me and very self-willed. He got through the money they left him in about five years, then started looking round for more. It never seemed to occur to him to work for it. I used to beg him to get a job. But he never did. I'm afraid he lived on women quite a bit when he was younger. He had studied chemistry and once tried to run a chemist's shop. Then he scrounged a living out of racing. He's never actually been to jail. But he was the type you read about in novels by Mrs Henry Wood. Drink and the devil, you know. Of course I was his sister, and that makes a difference.'

It was queer to see this noisy, hearty woman as she spoke of her brother. I was convinced that she was quite sincere.

'I tried, often enough. But for the last few years I've — well, I've tried to protect myself a bit. I told him I had no money left. I'd find him a pound or two when he came down. But then he'd go to the local pubs and make a fool of himself. Quarrel, you know.'

'Who with?' asked Beef. I've given up trying to correct his grammar.

Miss Shoulter paused.

'No one in particular,' she said. 'He just got quarrelsome. Anyone who argued with him.'

'You never heard of any particular quarrel?'

'No.'

'So he had no enemies down here?'

'Not that I know of.'

'Who did he know in Barnford?'

'Just the men he met at the Crown or the Feathers. And the Flipps, of course.'

'Why "of course"?'

'He'd known Flipp in London. There was some sort of business between them. I never knew that. It was through Ron that the Flipps came to live here at the beginning of the war. He told them about "Woodlands" being vacant. And whenever he was down here he went up to see Flipp.'

'They were friendly?'

'Yes. So far as I know. It's rather odd now I come to think of it, but I don't think I ever saw them together.'

'Who was aware that your brother was coming down for Christmas?'

'Pretty well everyone. He'd been down only three weeks before. He told several people then that he was going to spend his Christmas with me. And I probably told others.'

'I see. When he came down how did he usually come from the station?'

'He'd leave his bag for the bus to bring and walk up. Take the footpath through the wood.'

'He always did that?'

'Yes. It saves over a mile.'

'So that almost anyone living round here would know that some time or other after the arrival of the London train he would be walking along that footpath?'

'Yes, but they wouldn't have much idea of when. My brother usually stopped in the village for a drink and might easily not come here till they slung him out at ten o'clock.'

'Ah! Now about the gun.'

'Can't be much use over that, I'm afraid. Haven't the remotest when it went. I'm pretty careless about things, and there's nothing in this bungalow worth pinching except the dogs. I never noticed it had gone till a week before Christmas.'

'Do you think your brother might have taken it when he was last here?'

'Possible. But I shouldn't think so.'

'Who knew what cartridges you used?'

'Warlock's, I suppose. And I tell you who else knew that,' she said, smiling. 'Little Mr Chickle. He's a dear little man who's just come to live at "Labour's End". He was asking me about a fortnight ago where he could get some cartridges and I told him that his only hope was Warlock's and that they supplied "Fesantsure" to all of us.'

'Do you know him well?' asked Beef with a monstrous affection of casualness.

'Little Chickle? He's in and out of the house all day.'

'He does a bit of shooting, too?'

'Well, he *does*. But I don't honestly think he likes it. I think he sees himself as a country gentleman walking about with a gun. Poor little chap kept a watchmaker's shop for thirty years and has just retired. Pathetic, really. He told me the first time I saw him that he didn't shoot. He couldn't bear to cause suffering to a living creature. Then later he started this potting at rabbits.'

'I see. Now about these shots.'

'I can tell you exactly what I heard. I've gone over it so many times with the police that I should know by now. I heard two shots in quick succession somewhere between three and half-past, and two more just like them about an hour later. That's all."

'Where were you round about six?'

'Here. Why?'

'Didn't hear anything then?'

'No. I had the wireless on softly though.'

'You went to Copling in the afternoon?'

'Just to post a letter.'

'Who to?'

'My bank in Ashley.'

'Ask them if they've kept the envelope. Might have in these days of paper-saving. The envelope would be handy.'

'I will.'

'Then I think that's all.'

'There's one thing I ought to tell you.'

'Yes?'

'It's about Flipp. Very odd. When I was on my way to Copling a little before four o'clock I went to call on Flipp. I wanted to borrow something. And he wasn't in his house. I shouldn't have thought anything about it only he told the inspector that he'd never been out. I *know* he wasn't there. I went right in and called him and looked in the rooms. It was all open to the world – we leave our houses like that round here. And he wasn't in.'

'That's interesting,' said Beef. 'That *is* interesting. Now I'd just like a word with your kennel-boy.'

'Certainly. You'll find him down at the kennels. And for goodness' sake find out who *did* do it,' said Miss Shoulter as she showed us out. 'I hate all this suspicion about the place.'

'I will,' promised Beef. 'It may take time, but I will.'

'Good man!' shouted Miss Shoulter heartily.

CHAPTER ELEVEN

Mrs Pluck Could Shoot

JACK RIBBON, smartly attired in riding breeches and a yellow roll-top pullover, was waiting for us.

'Thought you'd want to see me,' he said.

'Oh, you did? And how did you know anything about us?' asked Beef.

'I heard you were about. Working for the old girl, aren't you?'

'That's not the way to talk of your employer,' admonished Beef. 'And who told you I was investigating on her behalf?'

'She said she'd engaged you. But it's all over the place you was on the job. Staying at the Crown, I hear.'

I could not help being amused at this when I remembered how indiscreetly Beef had spoken to Tom, Dick, and Harry about our business. I gave him a meaning look which he pretended to ignore.

'You hear a great deal too much,' remarked Beef. 'Perhaps all you know about this murder's hearsay, too?'

'Murder, is it?' said Jack Ribbon, sticking his hands in the high pockets of his breeches. 'Well, I'm not surprised. Nobody liked him and that's a fact.'

'Which means *you* didn't?'

'No, I didn't. But nor didn't nobody else. Scrounging blighter.'

'Who else didn't like him?'

'No one didn't.'

Ribbon refused to disentangle himself from this maze of negatives by enlarging on this, so Beef tried another question.

'Who did he associate with down here?'

'Anyone who'd buy him a drink.'

'No one in particular?'

'He always used to call on Flipp when he came down.'

'Always?'

'Never missed.'

'What time of day would he call?'

'Night-time, usually.'

'How do you know, then?'

For the first time Jack Ribbon showed some hesitation.

'Well?'

'There's a couple of young ladies work for Flipp.'

'You mean the servants? For Gawd's sake call a spade a spade, lad. There's nothing to be ashamed of in being a servant. "Young ladies who work for Flipp." Do you describe yourself as the young gentleman in charge of Miss Shoulter's kennels?'

'Well, servants, then. They told me.'

'Thick with them, are you?'

'I meet them at dances.'

'What else did they tell you?'

'Something I bet you'd like to know,' said Jack Ribbon with a grin.

'Come on, then,' said Beef.

'I'm keeping that to tell the real police.'

I thought Beef would lose his temper. But he showed some of his countryman's cunning.

'That's all right, then,' he said, turning over the page of his note-book as though he had finished with the matter. 'I'll tell Inspector Chatto you have some information for him, and I shall get it from him.'

Jack Ribbon's pleasant face fell.

'I was only thinking in terms of five bob,' he said blandly. Beef grinned.

'Young monkey. Ought to be ashamed of yourself trying to make money out of something you know in a case like this. Still, I was glad of five bob when I was your age.' And he handed him the money.

'It's not much really,' admitted Jack Ribbon. 'If you don't think it's worth the dollar you can have it back. It was about the girls going home for Christmas. Mrs Flipp's away, see, and they didn't want to go. Neither of them didn't. They've not much of a home and their father's a proper –'

'Now then!' warned Beef.

'Well, he is. And they'd much rather of stayed at "Woodlands" over Christmas. Besides, they're a decent pair of janes and didn't want to see the old man with no one to look after him at Christmas time. But he insisted that they went. Quite nasty he got. And in the end he paid their bus fares, too. Told them not to come back before the 27th.'

'Mm.'

'Worth the money?' asked Jack Ribbon.

'You can keep your dollar,' Beef said shortly. 'Now what else do you know?'

'I know a lot,' Jack said.

'Go ahead, then.'

Jack launched into a long discursive account of Ron Shoulter's visits, his drunkenness, and how he 'upset' Miss Shoulter, including the astonishing occasion on which he had found her in tears. He went on to the gun which he had not seen since he cleaned it back in October, adding that he did not often go into the house and in any case probably would not have noticed if it had gone. He did not think that Shoulter would have taken it 'unless he meant to sell it.' He had never known Miss Shoulter to use the gun and had never fired it himself. He knew Joe Bridge who was 'all right', though an awkward chap to fall out with. He did not suspect anyone in particular of murdering Shoulter.

About his finding the body. He had been on his way to church.

'Roman Catholic?' asked Beef.

'Yes. Midnight Mass at Copling.'

And he described with a slickness that suggested that he had told the story many times already his finding of the body. But Beef was not interested in the 'horror' aspect of this and wanted to know exactly how the corpse had lain. After several unsuccessful attempts at verbal explanation Jack Ribbon was induced to risk soiling his clean breeches and pullover by lying in the position in which Shoulter had been found, with a stick beside him for the gun. The dead man, it seemed, had been flat on his stomach with his face turned towards the fallen tree and his arms spread out.

He next told us of his midnight visit to Wellington Chickle, whom he described as a 'decent old boy'.

'You say the old man had gone to bed and the house-keeper was still up?'

'Yes. She'd been to the pictures at Ashley.'

Then he went on with the story of his call on Constable Watts-Dunton and how the latter's wife thought he was playing the fool.

'Why?' asked Beef severely.

'Well, what would you think if someone was to wake you up on Christmas night and say there was a dead man in Deadman's Wood?' asked Jack Ribbon, grinning.

'Depends whether whoever woke me up was known for larks or not. Larks on the police, I mean to say.'

Jack Ribbon was sobered by that, but enjoyed himself again in describing his walk with the solemn Watts-Dunton to the scene of the crime, and how the constable had remained on duty there while he, Ribbon, had gone for the doctor and to phone on Watts-Dunton's behalf to the Ashley police.

'Never got to Mass that night,' he added, 'and never got any sleep at all.'

'Too bad,' said Beef without any sign of sympathy. He had only a few more questions for Ribbon. The latter remembered Miss Shoulter going off on her bicycle in the direction of Copling at about four o'clock that afternoon, but did not see her return. She was back, however, when he 'packed up' at half past five. He recalled spontaneously that old Mr Chickle had seemed very put out when he had heard that the body had been found near the fallen tree, the spot where he had been known to hang about, and had also seemed a bit peeved by the news that the dead man was Miss Shoulter's brother. But Jack remembered the brandy with appreciation. He also recalled the occasion on which he had overheard Flipp tell Miss Shoulter about Chickle frequenting the spot by the fallen tree.

One last rather back-handed little story he told about Mrs Pluck, which I appreciated more than Beef because it seemed to give me another suspect. One day when old Chickle had been away in London he had been passing 'Labour's End' when Mrs Pluck had called him in for a cup of tea. He had been sitting in the kitchen with her when she remarked that she hated being left alone in the house. Surely she wasn't afraid of burglars, he had said, because he had noticed that she was strong as a horse and had hands like a man. Well, she had explained, it was lonely there by the wood when the old gentleman was away. Still, she had gone on with more spirit, if anyone did try anything she'd know what to do. Mr Chickle's gun was handy and she would not hesitate to use it. Jack had laughed and said he did not suppose she knew how to fire a gun, but she had told him not to be silly. She was a farmer's daughter and had shot rabbits before he'd been thought of. Then she had smoked a cigarette with him, which action, he said, 'looked funny'.

At last Beef seemed ready to go. I was frankly impatient, and when we had left young Ribbon I suggested that we should have to hurry to be in time for the inquest.

'No need to start careering along like that,' said Beef irritably. 'What do you want to go to the inquest for?'

I was dumbfounded.

'But of course we must go to the inquest,' I told him. 'There may be valuable information.'

'Valuable my foot,' said Beef in his grossest way. 'What you mean is you hope to fill a chapter with it.'

This was a particularly irritating remark, as I *had* hoped, as a matter of fact, that the inquest would be interesting enough to be included in my account of the whole affair.

'I've noticed that when you fellows want to make your story go further you always put in the inquest. What for? Nothing ever comes out that you don't know already. Yet you spin it out and describe all the witnesses and introduce the coroner, and all the time kid your readers they're learn-ing something more about the crime.'

'Beef!' I cried angrily. 'Who's writing this story, you or me?'

'I've got an interest in it, haven't I? I want you to make it readable. Let's get on with the investigation and leave out all that nonsense in the village hall. There's plenty that will interest your readers if you go about it the right way.'

'I shall do nothing of the sort,' I said. 'Whether you attend the inquest or not, I shall certainly do so.'

'All right. Keep your hair on. I'll have a bite of lunch and perhaps forty winks this afternoon. Helps me to think. You go and hear what the experts have to say.'

I did. And it is annoying to confess that as usual Beef was right. The proceedings were long and tedious, but I learnt nothing from them which I had not known already. Chatto had given us the gist of the experts' reports and hearing these in detail did not help. Miss Shoulter gave evidence of identification, Jack Ribbon was reproved when he tried to make our flesh creep with his account of his discovery and Wellington Chickle, Mrs Pluck, Miss Shoulter, and Mr Flipp were called on briefly to describe their hearing of the gun-shots. The coroner made a verbose summing-up and the verdict, as Beef and Chatto had predicted, was 'Murder against some Person or Persons Unknown'.

It was striking half-past four as I reached the Crown in a very bad temper, which was not improved when I went to Beef's room and found him stretched on the bed, fully dressed except for his boots, and snoring lustily.

CHAPTER TWELVE

Mr Chickle Heard Shots

AFTER tea Beef suddenly decided to call on Wellington Chickle and set off at a swinging pace towards 'Labour's End' while I told him about the inquest. It did not take us long to reach the house and we found ourselves on the doorstep under the scrutiny of Mrs Pluck.

'I don't know whether Mr Chickle will see you,' she said. 'He's very upset by this nasty business. He's not in just now, anyway.'

'When will he be back?' asked Beef.

'Well, he won't be long. He's having his afternoon stroll as usual.'

'Then we'll wait.'

Mrs Pluck seemed undecided.

'Mr Chickle does not like me to refuse anyone to come in,' she explained. 'But he's been so upset since this happened that I don't really think you ought to worry him. Such a tender-hearted old gentleman, it's cut him to the quick, happening right on his doorstep as you might say. Couldn't you ask me anything you want to know?'

'I'm afraid I must see Mr Chickle,' said Beef.

'Then you'd better come in and wait. I know he'll say I ought to have asked you, but I don't like to think of him being more upset than what he is. You'd never believe a thing like this could make such a difference to a man. Before it happened he was as cheerful as you please and now you'd scarcely know him. I'm quite worried about him.'

She had shown us into a comfortable book-lined room in which there was a bright fire.

'Better sit down, then,' she said. 'He won't be long.'

And she left us.

My eyes, wandering round the room, fell on something which made me give a cry of excitement.

'Look, Beef! What do you think of that?' And I pointed to the little table by the fire. On it, laid open at a page about half-way through the book, was a copy of *Case with Ropes and Rings*.* Beef stared at it with almost as much surprise as I had shown.

'That's interesting,' he said quietly and lapsed into thought.

'Don't you tell me again that I don't give you publicity. You're known even in Barnford!'

But he was not listening. He had risen from his chair and was making a thorough investigation of the books on Mr Chickle's shelves. He went from row to row slowly and methodically until he had examined the lot.

'Yes,' he murmured absently. 'Very interesting indeed.'

Just then the front door slammed and in a moment little Mr Chickle was with us. While he was greeting Beef I examined him carefully. Small, grey-haired, with a high dome of forehead and trim country clothes, he looked just what he was – a retired watchmaker. He was smiling now, but looking at his pink face I searched for any sign of the 'worry' that Mrs Pluck had mentioned. There was a rather strained and furrowed look about him, but for all I knew that might be habitual. I decided that now at any rate, whatever he may have been before, he did not look a happy man.

'Delighted. Delighted,' he was saying smugly. 'I know all about you, of course.' He nodded at the open copy of *Case with Ropes and Rings*. 'Edith Shoulter told me she had engaged you. I was wondering when you'd come to call on me.'

Beef also looked down at the novel.

'Interested in crime?' he asked.

'The merest amateur,' beamed Mr Chickle. 'We old retired fellows want something to occupy our minds. Though I have my garden, of course.'

* *Case with Ropes and Rings*. The Story of Sergeant Beef's Fifth Case. By Leo Bruce. (Ivor Nicholson and Watson.)

I may have been wrong, but I thought I detected some stress or effort behind this amiability. However, his words were friendly enough.

'What about some tea?' he asked.

'Just had ours,' said Beef.

'Sure? No? Then you won't mind if I sip a cup while we're chatting.'

'Did you attend the inquest to-day?' asked Beef.

'I did. And I must say I was surprised at the evidence. We had all taken it to be suicide, you know. One gathers that he had been a rather worthless fellow. When murder was proved so conclusively by the experts I was quite taken aback.'

'Experts can make mistakes,' said Beef.

'You incline to that view? Well, who knows? It may be that the police will revert to it, too.'

'Did you know the deceased well, Mr Chickle?'

'Never met him before in my life,' said Chickle lightly, then stopped.

'Before what?' asked Beef so quickly and quietly that even I was surprised.

'Before . . . well, a manner of speaking, of course.' Chickle spoke almost as quickly and calmly as Beef had done. If the question had shaken him he soon recovered. 'I haven't met him now, I'm afraid, in any true sense. Just seen the poor fellow carried past on a stretcher with his head covered, and that from no nearer than my windows. A most distressing sight.'

'And Miss Shoulter?'

'Oh, very well. We are excellent neighbours – frequently in one another's houses. A good and a plucky woman. Devoted to her dogs.'

'I believe you're very good to dumb creatures, too, Mr Chickle?'

'No more than most Englishmen, I believe.'

'Yet you once told Miss Shoulter that you were so afraid of hurting them that you disapproved of shooting.'

This time I am sure he was taken off his guard. I did not

know what was implicit in the question to disturb him, but for the first time he was confused.

'I told her . . . Oh, yes. That's perfectly accurate. It was when I first came here. I had heard about her kennels and thought she might be one of these animal cranks. You know, anti-vivisectionists and so on. And I did not wish to offend her susceptibilities. I have an almost morbid dislike of offending people. So I gave her the notion that my principles were the same as I supposed hers to be. When however she mentioned that she had a gun I realized that I need not be afraid of upsetting her, and admitted to my taste for shooting – the only sport I have ever much cared about.'

'Ah,' said Beef. 'You don't mind my asking questions that don't always seem to make sense, do you, Mr Chickle?'

'Oh, not in the least. Please ask anything you like. I must own that I cannot *quite* understand why you should take an interest in a remark made by me nearly a year ago to Edith Shoulter, but no doubt you have your reasons. We laymen must not expect to see into the trained mind, must we?'

Beef's next question was as surprising to me as it was to Mr Chickle.

'What made you come to Barnford?' he asked.

'Well, I was looking for a small country place and heard of this.'

'How did you hear of it?'

'Really! What *possible* relevance –'

'I'm sure you won't mind answering.'

'Well, no, I don't. As long as you're not pulling my leg. As a matter of fact I just came down and found it.'

'What made you come here? Did you know someone here? Had you been here before? Or did someone write and tell you that this bungalow was vacant?'

'I had passed through here on a walking tour some years previously. I remembered it as a pleasant village. I came down, found the bungalow, and bought it.'

'I see. You employed a solicitor for the transaction, I suppose?'

'No. As a matter of fact I didn't.'

'Don't like solicitors perhaps?'

'Nothing of the sort. There was no need for a solicitor. The estate agents had all the documents as drawn up when the previous tenant purchased. Actually I have a great respect for the Law.'

'Know any local solicitors?' asked Beef.

'I know Mr Aston who lives at Copling and has his office in Ashley. In fact he has just drawn up a new will for me. But aren't we wandering from the point a little? I cannot see how all these quite personal questions have any bearing on poor Shoulter's death. What I ask myself in that connexion is what *motive* could anyone have? That would seem the salient point. I understood that the police always start with motive.'

'I think they *do*, generally,' Beef admitted. 'So you came here to retire, Mr Chickle?'

'I did indeed. After a long and obscure life as a tradesman –'

'Obscure?'

'I'm afraid so. Quite obscure. Why, the purchaser of my business . . .' A sudden angry flush lit Mr Chickle's face. 'The purchaser of my business has even changed the name of the shop.'

Once again Beef spoke his irritating thoughtful 'Ah!' and for a while there was silence.

'Well,' said Mr Chickle smiling, 'this is the strangest questioning of a witness I can ever remember reading – even among your exploits!'

'Think so?' said Beef. 'Then we'll get back to the usual. The afternoon of the crime. Could you tell us how you spent it?'

'That's more like it,' said Mr Chickle. 'That's the question I've been waiting for. I could certainly tell you. I did a little gardening, came in here and read or wrote for half an hour perhaps, and then at half past three –'

'Before that you heard two shots?'

'Yes. In quick succession. At about a quarter past three. My housekeeper, Mrs Pluck, knows the precise time, no doubt. Indeed, she was able to give it to the coroner. I cannot recall it to the minute. Say three-twenty.'

'Yes?'

'I had just given Mrs Pluck her little Christmas-box in fact. Poor woman, I'm afraid she's a lonely soul. She seemed very grateful. We were standing here when we both heard those shots.'

'Any idea where they came from?'

'Fairly distant, I think.'

'Might have been from the spot where the body was found?'

'It might well have been.'

'Then?'

'Then I did another ten minutes in the garden and took my little stroll.'

'Take your gun?'

'Yes. As usual.'

'Would you mind telling us which way you went?'

'Certainly. Instead of going through the wood I skirted it and kept in the open. I followed right round the edge of it till I reached the drive going up to Flipp's house, then returned. It was pretty rough going.'

'Meet anyone?' asked Beef.

'Only a hare. I let off both barrels at him but he got away.'

'That would have been nearly an hour after you'd started out?'

'Yes. I was on my way home.'

'What made you choose that direction, Mr Chickle? I understand that you usually took the pathway through the wood.'

'Not *usually*. I often went that way to Miss Shoulter's.'

'It has been remarked that the place where the murder was committed –'

'I *still* think it's premature to call it murder,' interrupted Chickle.

'That that place is a favourite spot of yours. Several people have met you there.'

Mr Chickle smiled.

'A convenient half-way resting point between my bungalow and Edith Shoulter's.'

'Yes. So it would be. Now about this other shot or shots at five past six . . .'

'Shot or shots. That's rather the point. I can't be sure. I think it was two barrels fired simultaneously or almost simultaneously. But I can't be certain of that, and nor can Mrs Pluck. But it or they were certainly at five past six. I had just gone into the garden to bring in the tools I had been using when I heard them. I came straight in and remarked to Mrs Pluck that someone must be poaching.'

'And where did it seem to you that the shot or shots came from?'

'Oh, in the wood. I can't say where.'

'About the same distance as the shot at three-twenty?'

'About, yes.'

Both Beef and Chickle seemed quite exhausted by this long and searching dialogue. But, knowing something of the way in which Beef's mind worked, I realized that he would not stop till he had asked every question he needed to ask, and gathered all the material he wanted. For all his seemingly haphazard methods, Beef had a curiously orderly mind.

'Now there are three people I'd like to ask you about,' said Beef. 'And then I've done. First of all your housekeeper, Mrs Pluck.'

'Came to me with excellent references about eight months back,' said Chickle. 'A farmer's daughter, I gather. Married a ne'er-do-well who left her with a small child. The girl is married now and comes occasionally to see her mother. Mrs Pluck was ten years housekeeper at Kingmead, the historic mansion on the other side of Ashley. Sir Gerald Cocker's place. She left it and I was lucky enough to get her because she wanted a quiet situation. She did not mind the work, but was tired of the worry and responsibility. She's a thoroughly reliable woman, most honest and satisfactory. A good cook, a little over-punctual, perhaps, with an eye that never leaves the clock, but altogether what is called a treasure.'

'Did she know Shoulter?'

'I should think it's *most* unlikely. I never heard her mention him.'

'Good. Now what about Flipp?'

'I know very little about him. I understand that he was a friend of the Shoulters before coming here. He goes to London about twice a week. A somewhat coarse and crude person, I find.'

'Do you know whether he saw much of Shoulter?'

'I've never seen them together.'

'Finally a farmer called Bridge.'

'A very violent young man!' exclaimed the benevolent Mr Chickle with unexpected emphasis. 'Very violent. I had a most acrimonious argument with him about a month ago. Some of his land adjoins my shooting rights and he accused me of poaching.'

'Did he threaten you?'

Mr Chickle smiled.

'He said he'd see me in hell, if that's a threat.'

Beef suddenly stood up. He did not thank our host or apologize for his catechism.

'That's all,' he said as he snapped his note-book to.

'I hope I've been of some use,' said Mr. Chickle.

'I'm sure you have,' I hastened to put in. For even if there was anything suspicious about him, I saw no point in letting him see it.

'I wonder,' said Beef, 'if this would be a convenient time for us to have a chat with Mrs Pluck?'

Chickle looked at his watch.

'Five-thirty,' he said doubtfully, 'and I have dinner at eight. I hope you won't keep her too long?'

'I don't think so,' said Beef. 'Perhaps we could go out to the kitchen?'

'Yes. Only I must ask you to finish by six-thirty at the latest. There's nothing worse than hurried cooking.'

CHAPTER THIRTEEN

Mrs Pluck Makes Revelations

MRS PLUCK seemed far less pleased to see us now that we were entering her own domain with the evident intention of questioning her. There was something almost sinister in the look she gave us as she told us grudgingly to sit down.

'I don't know what I can tell you, I'm sure,' she said. 'I told them at the inquest about the shots and you've heard that.'

'Quite a lot of questions for you, Mrs Pluck,' remarked Beef cheerfully after a glance at his note-book. 'And first of all I'd like to know a little about yourself.'

'About me? What do you mean?'

'Where do you come from, for instance?'

'Kingmead. I should have thought Mr Chickle would have told you. I was ten years –'

'Yes, but where was your home?'

'That's no business of yours and nothing to do with what you've got to find out about.'

'But you've got nothing to hide?'

'Never mind whether I have or whether I haven't. I'm not answering any questions about my home.'

'When were you married?'

'Twenty-three years ago. But what that –'

'What was your husband's name?'

'Look here – you be careful what you're saying!'

'Keep steady, Mrs Pluck, keep steady. If you've got nothing to hide you can answer a few plain questions.'

'Pluck, of course.'

'Where is he now?'

'I don't know and I'm sure I don't want to, and I don't know why you're raking all this up. He left me after a couple of years with a twelve-months-old baby.'

'And you've never seen him since?'

'Nor heard of him.'

'What happened to the baby?'

'What do you *think* happened to the baby? What usually happens to babies? She grew up, of course.'

'And now?'

'Married and settled at Frittingbourne — twenty miles from here.'

'When did you see her last?'

'About a month ago. Anything else you want to know about my family?'

'No. But I should like to know where you went to that night.'

'Which night?'

'The night of the murder.'

'Ashley. Pictures.'

'What picture did you see?'

'Tarzan.'

'Which Tarzan?'

'How should I know which Tarzan? It was a Tarzan picture, anyway. At the Odious.'

'How did you get to Ashley?'

'By bus.'

'Anyone you knew in the bus?'

'No.'

'Well, the conductor will remember you, anyway. Christmas Eve, and that. Only small buses, aren't they?'

Mrs Pluck seemed doubtful for the first time.

'It's driver and conductor all in one in our buses. Don't see how he could remember.'

'He will. Now you said this afternoon that Mr Chickle had changed. Since when? When did you first notice it?'

'Well, he seemed a bit funny that afternoon, Christmas Eve, I mean, when he came in from his walk.'

'In what way?'

'Well, snappy like. He'd always been such a nice-spoken gentleman. He spoke quite sharp about his tea.'

'Ah.'

'And ever since then he's not been himself. Gloomy, like.

Never a smile. And doesn't sleep at night. I can hear him
moving about.'

'He was all right before this happened?'

'Yes. Funny, you know, in some ways. For ever asking the
time and what time he'd come and what time he'd gone.
Fortunately, I notice these things and was able to tell him
as often as not. Then he was queer about his garden.'

Now that we had left topics more personal to her and
were discussing her employer, Mrs Pluck became almost
garrulous.

'In what way queer about his garden?'

'For ever measuring this way and that, and shifting round
that line he used to plan paths and beds and what not, then
never giving any orders for them to be changed. Harold
Richey, who comes here two days a week to work, says it was
chronic. You better ask him about it, if you're that interested.'

Beef's note-book was out at once.

'Thanks,' he said, 'I will. Was he doing this measuring
and that on the day of the murder?'

'Was he *not*. First of all in the morning he had his old
line out shifting the pegs here and there and standing back
to see how it would look. That was on the village side of the
garden where the vegetable patch and a few ramblers are.
Then after lunch he was round on the wood side, where
there's a bit of lawn, stretching it out this way and that till
you wondered what he thought he was going to make. He
came in about half past two and I don't know whether he
played round with it any more before he went for his walk,
because I usually have five minutes to myself in the afternoon and my room's on the other side of the house –'

'Half a minute. Half a minute,' said Beef. 'You say you go
to your room in the afternoon. Yet you were with Mr Chickle at a quarter past three when the first shots were heard.'

'That was a bit different,' said Mrs Pluck. 'It was Christmas Eve and I knew he had a bit of a Christmas box for me.
I took it off to my room and did not come out again till it
was time to get his tea.'

'You didn't see him go off then?'

'No. My window faced towards Barnford. But I tell you what I *did* see not long after he'd gone.'

'What was that?'

'Young Joe Bridge with a gun under his arm going towards Barnford.'

'Towards Barnford?'

'Yes. He was then. Must have come down the footpath through the wood from Copling.'

'You did not see him on his way back?'

'No.'

'What about these shots?'

'I'm tired of going over them. There was the two at three-fifteen, and two more about half past four, and one more I heard with Mr Chickle at five past six.'

'*One* more?'

'Well, it sounded like one to me. Mr Chickle said it was two barrels let off almost at the same time. So it may have been.'

'Where did they come from?'

'So far as I could tell, the first and second lots were from some way away. The third sounded quite close.'

'Where were you for the third one?'

'In Mr Chickle's sitting-room making up the fire. He'd just gone out into the garden to take up his measuring line. Said someone might trip over it. He was always very careful of other people. And when the shots went he came in at once. "Someone poaching," he said. "Ah, well, we can spare them a rabbit or two." He was kind, mind you. I told him it sounded very near, but he said no, it was far away in the woods. I didn't argue about it, but I still think it was close at hand. Then he went out to finish bringing in his things. And that's all I can tell you.'

'H'm. There's still one or two things I must ask you, Mrs Pluck.'

'So long as you don't start on things you've no business to ask I'll tell you what I can.'

Beef leaned forward impressively.

'Did you know Shoulter?' he asked.

There was no doubt that the woman was flustered. I could see her great bony hands moving nervously.

'Shoulter?' she repeated, as though to gain time.

'Ron Shoulter, that was murdered,' amplified Beef.

'Never seen him in my life. Not till he was carried by on a stretcher. Then I only saw his feet.'

'Quite sure?' asked Beef. 'Far better speak out if you did.'

'No,' said Mrs Pluck. 'I never knew no Shoulter.'

'Then we'll leave that. Can you fire a gun?'

'No.'

'Ever tried?'

'No.'

'That's funny.'

'I don't see anything funny in it.'

'Have you ever said you could?'

'No.'

'You never told young Jack Ribbon, for instance, that you were a farmer's daughter and firing guns before he was thought of?'

'Did he say that? The young so-and-so. I'll tell him what I think of him – you see.'

'But is it true?'

'Course it's not true.'

'You're not a farmer's daughter?'

'Well, my father might have had a bit of land.'

'And you might have shot over it?'

'No harm in that, is there? A girl's as much right to do a bit of shooting as a man. Only when there's been a murder done with a shot-gun and you come and ask questions like that it's no wonder I'm careful what I say.'

'Then you can shoot?'

'I'm not saying I don't know how to. But I never have done. Not round here.'

'Thank you, Mrs Pluck,' said Beef, closing his note-book. 'Why, gracious me, it's past seven. Mr Chickle *will* be wild. He was afraid if I kept you too long you'd have to hurry over his dinner. We must go out the back way.'

We did. And for ten minutes as we groped our way back towards Barnford, Beef did not speak.

'Come on,' I said at last, 'what did you think of them?'

'I don't know what to think,' confessed Beef. 'It's a funny case, and no mistake. There's a lot of things I'd like to know. Why, for instance, did Chickle tell Miss Shoulter that he didn't like shooting? And what was Joe Bridge doing on that path that afternoon?'

'We'd better ask him,' I suggested.

'No. We won't do that. Joe Bridge will tell us everything in time.'

'Not if you don't go and question him.'

'I think he will,' said Beef obstinately.

'Why? Why should he incriminate himself? He did not tell the police he was on that footpath that afternoon.'

'But he'll tell me,' persisted Beef. 'Just you wait and see.'

I plodded on in silence.

'Yes, he'll come,' said Beef thoughtfully. 'Ever hear of Mahomet and the mountain?'

And since it was opening time when we got back I was pretty sure that that was all I should get out of him for that night.

I retired early and was just dropping off to sleep when Beef came into my room. I could see at a glance that he was flushed and talkative from the alcohol he had consumed in the bar downstairs. I admit that he never gets drunk, but in his present condition he could certainly be described as 'happy'.

'I've seen Richey,' he announced, gripping the foot of my bed for support.

'Richey?' I asked sleepily. 'Who's Richey?'

'Odd job man. Does a bit of gardening for Chickle. Says the old man's always playing round with his line and two pegs, and never decides anything. Richey privately thinks Chickle's a bit weak in the head. Says he's been fooling round for a fortnight now with his line and has not made a single change in the garden. He went up there on Boxing

Day and old Chickle hadn't planned a thing. Not a thing. What d'you think of that?'

I decided to tell Beef exactly what I thought.

'You barge into my room half intoxicated –' I began.

'Who's half intoxicated?'

'And wake me up to tell me a bit of nonsense like that. I think it's –'

'You don't think it's important, then? What I've just told you?'

'No!' I shouted.

Beef gave his hoarse laugh.

'Good night,' he said, and reeled off to bed.

Elevenses with the Curate

'I SHALL be glad when we finish with these interrogations,' said Beef next morning.

'So shall I,' I agreed fervently. 'What we need is to *do* something and not so much chit-chat.'

'There you go, thinking of your book all the time. What I want is to find out who is the murderer, not give entertainment to one or two lending library subscribers. However, there's only two more for now.'

'Who are they?'

'First this curate's sister, and then Flipp. And I shouldn't be surprised but what we find out something important from each of them. We'll see Miss Packham this morning, as soon as I've gone through my notes.'

It was eleven o'clock before we reached the little house on the outskirts of the village in which Mr Packham and his sister lived. The former was Curate-in-Charge of Barnford, which belonged to a parish nearer Ashley. He seemed to be fairly popular in the place, it being said that he 'didn't interfere'. We had gathered that he was agreeable to dances being held in the village hall and had no objection to cricket matches on Sunday. But I was not greatly impressed by his appearance when he opened the door. He was a large young man with a big white shining face, a skin of lard, and bright red ears. He had his mouth full when he appeared and there were cake crumbs on his black shirt front.

'My sister? Yes. Come in. We're just having our elevenses.'

His sister was as beefy as he was porcine, a weather-beaten young woman in a hand-knitted jumper.

'Have a cup of coffee?' she suggested. 'And try these cakes. Given us yesterday.'

She handed the plate to Beef who refused, saying something about 'eating between meals'.

'If you can get the meals,' she said, biting at another rock-cake. 'It's so difficult nowadays. Rationing hit Edwin very hard, I'm afraid.'

Rev. Edwin Packham seemed determined to make up for this now.

'You're trying to solve this mystery, aren't you?' he mumbled, showering fragments of pastry over himself. 'Working for Miss Shoulter, I understand?'

'That's it,' said Beef.

'How are you getting on? Plenty of suspects?'

'Too many, I'm afraid,' I interjected.

'Still, you'll sort it all out in the end, I expect,' said Miss Packham comfortably. 'Now what on earth can you want to know from *me*, I wonder. I didn't even know Miss Shoulter's brother.'

'I want you to recall your last Jumble Sale,' said Beef.

'Great success,' said Mr Packham. I wished he wouldn't use so many sibilants while he was eating. 'And I won the cake weighing competition.'

'Congratulations,' said Beef. 'I understand that you had an old clothes stall, Miss Packham?'

'I did. And I sold every stitch. With clothing coupons and so on it wasn't difficult.'

'I'm going to ask you to try to recall one particular item sold,' said Beef seriously.

'I'll try.'

'It was a pair of shoes belonging to Miss Shoulter.'

In spite of our sober faces there was a sudden roar of laughter from the two of them.

'Edith Shoulter's shoes!' cried Miss Packham at last. 'I wondered what *on earth* I'd do with them. *Have* you seen her feet? They're *gigantic*. Size twelve, I should think, if they have any size as large as that. They tell me policemen have big feet. I always say Edith Shoulter ought to join the Women's Constabulary!'

'And what did you do with them?' asked Beef when a fresh burst of laughter from the curate and his sister had subsided.

'Well, what *could* I do? I couldn't refuse them; it would
have offended the poor woman. So I made up a basket of old
shoes and put hers in with the rest. Then I sold it as a Lot.'

'Who bought it?' asked Beef grimly.

'Who did buy it? Do you remember, Edwin?'

I could see that Beef was almost holding his breath in the
anxiety of the moment. It was evident that he attached the
greatest importance to this query.

'I'm sure I don't remember,' said the curate. 'I was looking
after the fruit and vegetables.'

'It wasn't Mrs Flipp, I *know*,' said Miss Packham.

'I hope you'll manage to remember,' said Beef. 'It's most
important.'

'But why? What in the world can Edith Shoulter's outsize
shoes have to do with her brother's murder?'

'These things cannot always be explained,' I pointed out.
'You may be sure that if Sergeant Beef says it is important
it *is* important.'

Mr Packham took the last cake.

'You told me you sold the lot in an old clothes-basket,' he
said.

Suddenly there was a shriek from his sister.

'I remember! I remember perfectly clearly now. I can't
think how I came to forget. It was our dear little Mr Chickle
who bought the whole collection. He'd seen a pair of carpet-
slippers of my brother's which he wanted. You remember
those carpet slippers, Edwin? Old Miss Sant back in Horn-
sey made them for you and you never would wear them. My
brother hates being given that sort of thing by parishioners,
and Miss Sant was a butcher's sister and could easily have
sent us a leg of mutton. They were almost new and I put
them in with the rest and little Mr Chickle fancied them.
Just right for him, too. So I rather wickedly made him buy
the lot, poor man.'

'Did he take them all away? Or just his slippers?'

'No. He took the lot. I made rather a good joke about it,
I remember. I asked him if he was going to grow boot-trees
in his garden! Boot-trees, see?'

And there was another hearty laugh from the brother and sister.

'Very funny,' said Beef politely. 'And he took the whole lot?'

'Yes. Richey was at the Sale, and he does a few days' work each week for Mr Chickle. About the only work he does do. The rest of the time he's in the Crown. And little Mr Chickle called him over to the stall and asked him to bring the basket up next day. Seven pairs, he said, *and* the basket. Well, you have to be like that with Richey.'

'Thanks,' said Beef.

'I could tell you a very funny story about our little Chickle,' said the curate.

I had really had more than enough of the Packham humour and said that really we ought to be going. But Beef grinned and asked what that might be.

'It's about eight months ago now,' said Mr Packham. 'Bluebell time. The whole of Deadman's Wood becomes carpeted with bluebells, a really gorgeous sight. I was walking through on my way to Copling and had just reached the very spot at which Shoulter's body was found. I happened to glance over the fallen tree there, and what *do* you think I saw?'

It was quite clear that the curate was preparing to give us the laugh of our lives. He could scarcely contain his own mirth.

'Little Mr Chickle!' he roared. 'Crouched down behind the tree like a rabbit and peeping over the top at me! I could scarcely believe my eyes. He looked so funny. Like something out of *A Midsummer Night's Dream*. "Picking bluebells?" I asked him, and he said he was. His suit was covered with mud and dead leaves.'

Mr Packham and his sister seemed in no hurry to see us away, and Beef leaned back in his chair comfortably.

'Do you know this Mr Flipp at all well?' he asked.

'I know Mrs Flipp better,' said the curate's sister. 'She's a good soul and very helpful in the village. They keep a lot of poultry, you know.'

'Excellent birds,' put in Mr Packham with gusto. 'Splendid layers and good roasting fowl.'

'What about Mr Flipp?'

'We don't know him very well,' said Miss Packham.

'We don't know him at all well,' said Mr Packham stiffly.

'Anything wrong?' asked Beef.

'No – o. Nothing really. We find him rather a coarse individual. Language and so on.'

'That's all?'

'Well, there was one tiny thing I didn't like just at Christmas time,' Miss Packham remarked. 'It showed, I'm afraid, that he isn't quite truthful. You see we managed to get hold of some Christmas cards and sent them out on the evening of the 23rd. And when I called on Mr Flipp on Boxing Day I noticed that although he had quite a display of Christmas cards on his mantelpiece ours was not amongst them. I asked him about it, and he said he had never received it. He spoke with such violence that I felt sure he was not speaking the truth. He got quite worked up about it, complained of inefficient postal service, and repeated again that he had never received our card. Now I happen to know that that was an untruth.'

'How do you know?'

'Well, I asked the postman. In a small place like this everyone at the post office knows everyone else's business, besides when they take the lonely roads I expect the postmen take a peep at postcards and open letters. The postman remembered my card perfectly well. He delivered it on Christmas Eve – it was the only letter for Mr Flipp by that post. He says he met Mr Flipp at the gate and handed it to him. Mr Flipp put it in the pocket of his mackintosh as soon as he had glanced at it, and marched off.'

'What time would that be?'

'Well, he came here about half past two that day. I think it was an extra delivery. Didn't he, Edwin?'

'That's right. Brought that parcel of sweets from Betty Clough.'

'Ours is almost the last house he would call at before he

went up to Deadman's Wood. So it must have been before three when he got there.'

'And Mr Flipp was going out?'

'So the postman said. He was dressed to go out. But he only saw him making his way to the mixing shed by his chicken run, which is between his house and the wood.'

'Well, I'm very very grateful to you for all your help and information,' said Beef.

'I only hope we've been of some use,' said the curate. 'I'm afraid we've just given you a lot of gossip. My sister and I cannot help seeing the funny side of things, you know. If you had *seen* little Chickle squatting down behind that tree I'm sure you'd have roared!'

Both the curate and his sister laughed for some time over this pleasant recollection, but were recalled to sterner thoughts by a call from the butcher's. We left them having a heated debate in which 'rations', 'Offals', and 'extra' were words which seemed frequently to occur.

'Are you satisfied?' I asked Beef as we left the house.

'Yes, quite.'

'You don't seriously suspect little Chickle?' I asked.

'I should like to know what he did with those shoes.'

'Probably threw them away.'

'I hope so,' said Beef.

'What now?' I asked.

'We've just time to do Flipp before lunch. He's the last.'

CHAPTER FIFTEEN

Beef Borrows a Raincoat

I DID not like Flipp from the moment I saw him. A big brutal-looking man, he seemed both overbearing and cunning. I felt that he would have liked to be thoroughly rude to us, but that for some reason he dared not. He ought to have been greased and bloated with that face of his, but there was something oddly deflated about him as though he were a powerful and successful man who had suddenly lost his authority.

His home gave more evidence of prosperity than most of the houses we had visited, and he asked us into a large well-furnished room and offered us sherry.

'I've been expecting you to call on me,' he admitted. 'I've had the police here a couple of times, so I was prepared for the private detectives as well. And I suppose *you*'ll ask me all the same questions as they did – where I was that afternoon –'

'Where were you?' asked Beef.

'I thought so,' said Flipp. 'I was here. Never left the house.'

'Do you mean in the house? Or the grounds?'

'I mean the house. It was a beastly cold day and I sat over a fire with a kettle of hot water, a lemon, and a bottle of whisky to cheer me. Celebrating Christmas on my own.'

'I see. Yet the postman remembers you just going out.'

I thought that Mr Flipp would fly into a temper. But after a short pause he spoke quite genially.

'Been checking up on me already, eh? The postman is perfectly correct. He met me at the gate. As a matter of fact I was just going to feed the chickens when I saw him coming and waited. Then I went round to my mixing shed. To that extent I *did* leave the house.'

'Do you remember what the postman gave you? What came for you by that post?'

'Can't say I do. Nothing of importance, I think. Probably a circular or something.'

'Not a Christmas card?'

'Might have been.'

'You knew this man Shoulter well, I believe?' asked Beef after a stare at his note-book.

'We were neighbours in London,' said Flipp shortly.

Beef attacked his note-book.

'Where was that, sir?' he said.

After only a moment's hesitation Flipp said, 'I have a large commission agent's business in Gordon Street, Paddington. I still keep a controlling interest though it is now a limited company. Shoulter occupied the premises next door.'

'As a private house?'

'No. He had a small chemist's shop.'

'I see,' said Beef. 'How long ago was this?'

'Twelve years. He was only there for a year or so, then he sold the business and went in for professional punting. He was always fond of the horses.'

'So a friendship which started just by you being neighbours in business has lasted all these years?'

'Well, I was sorry for Shoulter. And for his sister. I've tried to help him on and off. But he was a fellow who would not help himself.'

'So I've gathered. You also knew Mr Chickle, I think?'

'Not very well. He's been here once or twice and I've met him at Edith Shoulter's. Seems a harmless little chap.'

'Met him anywhere else, sir?'

'Not that I can remember.'

'I believe you mentioned to Miss Shoulter that he had been hanging about at a certain spot in the wood.'

'Oh, that. You shouldn't take me too seriously, you know. I believe I met him once by that fallen tree and mentioned it to Edith Shoulter. Quite a casual meeting.'

'Ah. What was he doing there?'

'Doing? Nothing. He was just there.'

'I see. You have a gun, Mr Flipp?'

'I have.'

'What kind is it?'

'A twelve-bore.'

'When did you use it last?'

'About three years ago. I used to do a bit of duck shooting on some marshy land in Sussex, but I've had to give it up since nineteen-forty.'

'Would you have any objection to my seeing your gun?'

'Not the slightest. I'll bring it along.'

Beef examined the gun carefully, squinting down the barrel like an officer on an arms inspection in the army.

'Been cleaned recently,' he remarked.

For the first time Flipp showed irritation.

'Of course it has. I know how to look after a gun.'

'Yes. I see you do.'

Beef put the gun down and stood up.

'I've nothing more to ask you at present,' he said, and rather rudely made his way into the hall before our host could accompany us.

There was a queer little scene by the front door. When Flipp arrived Beef was already wearing a light-coloured raincoat which I am sure he had not had on when we arrived. Flipp stared at him for a moment.

'Isn't that my raincoat?' he said.

Beef examined it and then appeared abashed.

'Why, so it is!' he said. 'I'm sorry, Mr Flipp. I've got one just like it at home and took it without thinking.'

He replaced it on the peg and we took our leave

'Whatever did you do that for?' I asked.

Beef's voice became conspiratorial.

'Just as I hoped,' he said. 'One of the pocket linings is adrift.' And he chuckled to himself.

That afternoon we had a conference with Inspector Chatto in the small private room at the Crown, which chatty little Bristling arranged for us with a good deal of talkative pleasure.

'You sleuths want somewhere you can be quiet in, I know,'

he said. 'Well, when you want your tea, shout out. I suppose you'll be deciding who's guilty this afternoon?"

'That's most unlikely,' I told him. 'The investigation is still in its initial stages.'

'Oh, I see. Well, good hunting to you,' he smirked and scurried out to leave the three of us in conclave round the table.

'I've done my interrogation,' announced Beef. 'And I think there may be a few bits that are new to you. They've all been willing enough to talk, anyway.'

Referring to his note-book he went painstakingly over the information he had gathered from each of the persons he had seen. I watched Inspector Chatto, who made a few notes, and I gathered that the points which interested him chiefly, either because they were new to him or perhaps because they fitted a theory he had already formed, were these:

(1) *Miss Shoulter's shoes.* He went so far as to admit that the footprints found in the wood *could* have been caused by someone wearing these, though he would not commit himself to more than that. When he heard about the old pair sold to Wellington Chickle at the Jumble Sale he agreed again that this might be the pair. It would be necessary to find out what Chickle had done with them. Beef asked him if he would leave that to him for the moment as he had a theory about those shoes and did not want Chickle questioned just now. Chatto agreed, but warned Beef that it might be necessary in a few days to take it up. Beef would be given warning, though.

(2) *Miss Shoulter's story* of visiting Flipp's house and finding him out that afternoon interested Chatto profoundly and he thanked Beef for bringing it to light. He said it was very important for a reason he would explain later.

(3) *Ribbon's account* of how Flipp sent his servants away was also of paramount interest to Chatto. 'Of course,' he said, 'we should have got it in time as I'm going to see the two girls, but it's handy to have it from you first.'

(4) *The postman's story* of Flipp leaving the house that

afternoon Chatto characterized as second-hand, but took a note of it all the same. I could see that his interest was centred on Flipp, especially when he said that since Flipp went into the mixing shed that might well be where he kept his gun.

(5) *Mrs Pluck's ability to shoot* caused Inspector Chatto to smile in a slightly superior way, but he agreed that she 'needed looking into' and made a note that her alibi for Christmas Eve should be checked as far as possible.

(6) It seemed difficult to interest him in anything connected with Chickle. When Beef told him about Chickle's lie to Miss Shoulter about shooting he said it was 'natural enough in the circumstances'. After a wordy story by Beef about Chickle's garden measurements he merely asked what about it, and he seemed nearly as amused as the Packhams had been at the curate's story of Chickle crouching behind the fallen tree. Beef did not try to persuade him.

(7) When it came to Mrs Pluck's statement that she had seen Joe Bridge going down the footpath that afternoon, Chatto said he could soon get the truth of that from Bridge. Again Beef begged him to 'lay off' for as long as he could. Beef still seemed certain that if nobody questioned Bridge he would become so steamed up at being left alone that he would come and volunteer a statement. And one volunteer, proclaimed Beef, was worth six conscripts. If he had heard nothing from Bridge after five days, or if Chatto found it essential before that, he would be questioned.

Finally, when Beef began to touch on Flipp's account of his old acquaintance with Shoulter, Chatto stopped him.

'I know all about that,' he said. 'And a lot more. We've not been twiddling our thumbs, you know. I've got a bit of a story for *you* now!'

'That's good,' said Beef, and we both adopted attitudes of close attention.

CHAPTER SIXTEEN

Inspector Chatto's Theory

'We haven't been idle,' said Chatto. 'But as I told you, we've been working from another angle. Motive is what we looked for, and we've found it. Or more precisely, we've found someone here in the district who seems to have had a very strong motive for killing Shoulter. And that's something to start on.

'I need not go into all the inquiries we've made, or tell you how we've made them. The picture is fairly complete now, and what you've told me this afternoon goes a long way towards finishing it. A long way, but not right to the end. We've still got to get more direct evidence. But I don't think that will be difficult. My experience is that once you know your man the evidence piles up pretty quickly. All right. Here's the story.

'Shoulter, as you already know, has never been much good. As a boy at school the only subject in which he showed any interest was chemistry, and his parents, who seem to have indulged him in anything he took a fancy to, encouraged him to make a career of analytical chemistry. He played about with it for a bit, but never took his degree. Then he seems to have been at a loose end for a few years with an allowance from his father and mother. We've got a list of his associates at this time, and although none of them seem to have any connexion with Barnford, they were a pretty bad lot. Several of them have done terms of imprisonment since then.

'Shoulter gave himself out to be a bachelor. But one man who knew him at this time maintains that he had been married and had left his wife. We haven't any evidence of that yet, though I dare say it will be forthcoming in time. It's surprising how much you can find out of a man's life when you begin to dig into it.

'What we do know is that not long before the death of Shoulter's father the old man, in an effort to make Shoulter settle down, bought him a small chemist's shop in Gordon Street, Paddington. It wasn't much of a business and Shoulter did not improve the status of it, though he increased the takings. He added rather dubious books and goods to his stock and kept open at night. But he had not a good name in the neighbourhood. From the study of analytical chemistry to keeping a retail shop in Paddington was a bit of a drop, of course, but he had been right down in the meantime, and was lucky to get that chance, and he did not make much of it, as you shall hear.

'Next door to his shop was a bookmaker's called Monequick, Ltd. And here, I hope, is a surprise for you. The managing director's name was Philipson, and we have established that he was none other than our Mr Flipp of "Woodlands", Barnford. But it's more interesting than that.

'Philipson lived in Maida Vale and was unhappily married to an invalid wife. He was also known to be associating with a Miss Murdoch. This latter, we learned, had been the only daughter of a florist who had made a fortune and died leaving her three shops and a considerable sum of money, well invested. I say "considerable" since, although we have no exact figures, it is a fairly safe bet that Philipson would not have been interested in her unless her fortune was worth while. She was a pale mousy creature with little character and no personal attraction. Philipson seems to have dominated her without difficulty until she was prepared to follow him without question. But one thing she could not do – that was hand over her money to him in a lump. Her father had been a shrewd old man who had tied it up about as securely as money could be tied, and all she could lay hands on was the income. So *if* Philipson was to enjoy the florist's careful savings and investments he could only do so by marrying her.

'The set-up is clear, I hope, and not unfamiliar. And the story proceeds according to precedent. Mrs Philipson died suddenly from an overdose of morphine.

'Yes, there was an inquest, and quite a deal of scandal in the newspapers. It was never of course suggested that Philipson had murdered his wife – the law of libel is still an almighty thing. But newspapers went as near the mark as they dared and people who knew the couple did not hesitate to say it outright.

'I have read the whole inquest proceedings, and found them most interesting. The post-mortem had revealed the poison all right – the quantity in about five doses. But the doctor who had been attending Mrs Philipson was quite positive about the number of tablets he had prescribed for her, the number he had given Philipson to give her, and the number remaining. It was impossible, he said, for her to have had more than the normal dose from the quantity held by her husband. He had given her *one* tablet on the evening before she died and three remained. This was as it should be.

'Philipson, too, was positive. The doctor had told him when and how to give his wife the morphine, and he had carried out these instructions to the letter. On the night of her death he had given her one tablet and that was all. He seemed very distressed by her sudden death, but he was able to tell the coroner quite a lot about Mrs Philipson's state of mind which was more or less corroborated by servants and relatives. It appeared that for many years the lady had been suffering from fits of melancholia and it was suggested that she had been in the habit of taking drugs before her illness. A servant spoke of some "tablets" she had seen in her possession, and although there was nothing to show that they had been anything more noxious than aspirin the impression was given that she might have kept concealed her own supply of morphine. At any rate there was an open verdict and Philipson found himself a widower and free to marry the pale and uninteresting Miss Murdoch. This he did about six months later, and has lived comfortably since then on her adequate income. She is, you will have realized, the present Mrs Flipp.

'Meanwhile Shoulter, who had been a keen if not a very

regular client of Monequick's, the bookmaking business of which Philipson had been managing director, spent more and more time racing and less in his shop until the chemist's business was in a bad way, and he began to look round for a purchaser. He never found one. He had probably allowed it to sink so far that it was worth no one's while to start building it up again. Eventually he sold the remnants of his stock and left the premises, which were taken over by a tobacconist-newsagent who is still there.

'Now that's the story as we've put it together from a number of reports, and there is only one thing to add to it – the most significant thing of all, perhaps, though it is still not conclusive. We find that Philipson, who by the way changed his name to Flipp when he came to live at "Woodlands", has been drawing from his bank over the last few years a series of those sums in small denominations which nearly always mean blackmail. You know – fifty or a hundred pounds at a time in one-pound notes every few months. They cannot very well mean anything else.

'But during the war years, since Flipp came to live at "Woodlands", these have increased alarmingly, on one occasion being as much as five hundred pounds. And as far as we can check up we find that these withdrawals coincided with the visits of Shoulter to his sister, during which visits, you will remember, he called on Flipp.

'The analogy is only too plain, and the instrument of blackmail is almost certainly the poison book which Shoulter must have kept when he had his little pharmacy. If we could lay hands on that I feel sure we should find an entry dated not long before the death of the first Mrs Philipson, which showed that Philipson had purchased and signed for a quantity of morphine. That, of course, is a broad outline. We have yet to interview the doctor who attended Mrs Philipson, since unfortunately he sold his practice and became a doctor on a big liner, then during the war joined the I.A.M.C., and is at present in India. We don't even know whether, if Philipson did sign for morphine, he did so in his own name, or whether Shoulter managed to sell it to him without a signature. But all this we shall clear up in time. So far as this end of the case is concerned, we've found a man with a motive, which is more than we had before, in spite of all your eccentric old watchmakers and quarrelsome farmers.

'There are some other interesting aspects to the story. Miss Shoulter was friendly with the Flipps. Did she know what her brother was doing? Did she take any part in it? Or was she to some extent and in some way another of Shoulter's victims? We know that she used to give him money.

'Then, where was Flipp that afternoon? He had got rid of his servants for the two days rather peremptorily, and there were no witnesses to his movements. The postman saw him at about three and Miss Shoulter states that he was not at home at four o'clock, so he has a very crucial period of time to account for. We know he has a gun which has been recently cleaned. It all begins to hang together nicely.

'Now then, Beef, let's hear what you think of it all. Are you going to admit that the case is getting strong against Flipp, or are you going to do what you private fellows are always supposed to do – pick someone quite different to the police suspect, and show the police where they're making a bloomer?'

Beef was sucking his moustache.

'No,' he said at last. 'I'm not going to do that, because I can't. Not at present, anyway. I can't see that you *are* making a bloomer. Things look very black against Flipp. Very black indeed. And if you find that poison book they will be more so. No, I've no holes to pick at all.'

'Thanks,' said Chatto cheerfully. 'And I admit that we've got nothing final yet. There's a good deal more spadework to be done both at the other end and this. We've got to prove that Shoulter was blackmailing Flipp. That ought not to be too hard. Then we've got to prove that Shoulter was killed by Flipp, and that may be very, very difficult. And in the meantime we shall not, of course, refuse to consider other possibilities even if they take us in quite new directions.'

Personally I thought that Beef was giving in far too easily. I believed that his line of research had given him quite different suspicions and I did not like the way he had conceded the probability of Chatto's case, which seemed to me a bit too plausible.

'One thing I'd like to mention,' I said defiantly, 'is the *place* of the murder. If Flipp shot Shoulter as you say, isn't it rather a coincidence that it should have happened at the very clearing in the woods where Mr Chickle was known to lurk?'

Beef gave this idea a noisy laugh.

'Lurk!' he shouted. 'You've been writing too many detective stories!'

I kept my temper.

'But *isn't* it?' I insisted.

It was Beef who silenced me, though it was his theory, I believed, that I was defending.

'No coincidence at all. We know from young Jack that Flipp had remarked on the old gentleman's hanging about round there. What more likely than that Flipp should have chosen the spot *for that very reason*? He knew that Mr Chickle might be out with a gun at that time. It would have been an easy way to divert suspicion to him.'

'Possibly,' I conceded.

'Any question you'd like to ask us?' Chatto asked Beef in an expansive way, as though he wished to recall the fact that he had all the resources of Scotland Yard behind him.

'Yes, there *is* one thing,' said Beef. 'You said it was believed that at some time Shoulter had been married and had left his wife. What evidence is there of this? Do you know the date or the woman's name?'

Chatto shook his head.

'I'm afraid not,' he said. 'It's only some second-hand information we picked up. But if you're seriously interested I've no doubt I could find out.'

'I am. Seriously interested.'

Chatto glanced at him.

'I wonder what you're up to now. Still, you've given me some useful stuff to-day, and I told you I'd repay your information with mine. I'll find out for you.'

'Thanks,' said Beef shortly, and the conference broke up.

CHAPTER SEVENTEEN

Joe Bridge at Last

BEEF's day has some curious landmarks. Where you and I speak of 'morning', 'afternoon', 'lunch-time', 'sunset', and so on, for Beef there are four points in the clock-round – morning and evening 'opening time' and 'closing time'. I have sometimes spoken to him about this. Even when we have been among the more respectable people with whom our cases have brought us in touch, Beef will glance at the clock and say: 'Well. It'll soon be "opening time". We must be running along.' Or, 'Well, if we don't hurry it'll be "closing time".' I try to explain to him that not everyone counts the hours by the licensing laws, and that these continual references to public-houses are not in good taste. But he is, of course, incorrigible.

At what he would have called 'closing time' that evening we had retired to the back room when Mr Bristling put his head in. He had just been bolting the outside doors.

'Young Bridge is waiting,' he said. 'Wants a word with you. He's had a few but he's all right. Bring him in, shall I?'

'There you are,' said Beef to me, not concealing his triumph. 'What did I tell you? I knew he'd be along.'

Young Bridge was six feet four and, I judged, would have been a handsome fellow if it had not been for the effect of too much beer-drinking during his years of manhood. His cheeks were of a coarse crimson texture, though there were remnants of good features noticeable. He pushed into the room with his hands in the pockets of his mackintosh, and I could see at once that Mr Bristling was not exaggerating when he said that Bridge had 'had a few'.

'Evening,' he blurted out in a gruff voice. 'You Sergeant Beef?'

'That's my name,' said Beef pompously.

'Well, I'm going to tell you something.'

'Wouldn't it be wiser for you to inform the police?'

'No. I don't want anything to do with the police.'

Beef coughed.

'Had some trouble perhaps?'

'Me? With that fellow Dunton? I shouldn't have trouble with his sort, I can tell you. No, what I've got to say I'll say to you and get it over with.'

He slumped into a chair.

'Why haven't any of you been to me?'

'Why should we?' asked Beef quickly.

Bridge did not like that.

'There's been a lot of talk,' he said lamely. 'I'm supposed to have been out for that —'s blood.'

'Which . . . ?'

'Shoulter.'

'Are you?'

'You know very well I am.'

'And were you "out for his blood"?'

'Well, I didn't like the fellow. But I didn't murder him.'

'That's what a good many say.'

Bridge hesitated.

'You knew I went down that path that afternoon, didn't you?'

'Yes.'

'Someone see me?'

Beef nodded.

'Well, as a matter of fact I go down that path almost every Saturday. I go to see my uncle and aunt in Barnford. But this time I had my gun.'

'Yes.'

'Then why haven't I been questioned?'

'I can't answer for the police. I haven't got round to you yet, myself.'

'Do you think I did it?'

'I don't know who did it.'

There was another pause.

'I decided to walk down to Barnford that afternoon,' Bridge said at last, rather sulkily. 'And I took my gun.'

'What for?'

'Why not? I had to cross several of my own fields. Might have got a dinner.'

'But you didn't?'

'No.'

'You never fired the gun?'

'No.'

'Is that what you've come to tell me?'

'No. There's more to it than that. I passed the Shoulter woman's kennels and took the footpath which enters the wood at her place and comes out by Chickle's. I did not meet anyone till I reached that little clearing where the body was found.'

'Go on.'

'Well, I didn't exactly meet anyone there. But just as I came into the place I heard some movement to my right, looked over and saw a man disappearing among the trees.'

'A man? Who was it?'

There was a breathless silence, then Bridge said that he didn't know.

'He was off pretty quickly and he didn't turn round. He seemed to be walking like a cat – half as though he didn't want to be seen, and half as though he didn't want to be heard, but most important of all to get out of the way. All I saw was that he was a biggish man wearing a raincoat.'

'Ah.'

A slow grin crossed Bridge's face.

'Interest you?' he asked.

'Yes.'

Then something in Beef's manner seemed to anger Bridge.

'It happens to be true!' he said shortly.

'I never said it wasn't.'

Bridge looked sulky for a few moments, then continued his story.

'I went on down the path,' he said, 'and about fifty or a hundred yards on I met Shoulter.'

'Did you speak to him?'

'No.'

'You'd had a bit of a row?'

'I had, and I didn't want to start it again, else I'd have knocked him to hell. I decided just to walk past. And he didn't seem to want any trouble because he made way for me on the path.'

'Was he carrying a gun?'

'He had his golf clubs with him. They were in one of those long mackintosh bags with a top to them. It could have been in there, I suppose. He wasn't carrying it otherwise.'

'And he passed straight on?'

'Yes.'

'That would have been about three-fifteen?'

'Roughly. Soon after he passed there was a shot from the wood. I knew that little Chickle had what he called the "shooting rights" there and thought it was him potting at a stray pheasant. But it wasn't.'

'How do you know?'

'Because a few minutes later I came to his bungalow and saw him in the garden.'

'The devil you did. Sure it was him?'

'Certain. I saw his face.'

'Did he see you?'

'No. I took good care he shouldn't. I'd come down the path quietly and looked into his garden from behind cover.'

'Why?'

'Well, I caught him poaching once, and I didn't want him to accuse me of the same thing.'

'Just because you were carrying a gun on a public foot-path?'

'Yes. I'd just come through the wood, after all, and there had been a shot a few minutes before.'

'Ah. And did you see him?'

'Yes. He was in his garden. I watched him for a few minutes. And I saw something very odd.'

'Mm?'

'At least,' said Bridge in a rather more friendly and confidential tone than he had been using, 'it may not seem odd to you, and it may not have any meaning, as it were. But it seemed funny to me. He had a line in his hand like a gardener uses for laying out paths and beds. He had one end of it pegged by the window and was walking round with the other end as though he couldn't decide where to put it. Then I saw him go across his little piece of lawn to where it goes up close to the wood. He stood there for a moment, then looked all round him, over to the windows of the house and towards where I was standing in a furtive sort of way. Then he stooped down and tied the end of his line to what looked like a thinner line already lying there.'

'He did, did he?' said Beef, staring, rather vacantly I thought, at Bridge.

'Yes. What was the idea?'

Beef was silent.

'I don't know for certain,' he said at last.

'But you've got some sort of a theory?'

'Might have,' said Beef.

'And it fits in?'

'Yes. It fits very nicely. Almost too nicely. And now I'm going to give you a bit of advice. You go and tell your story, exactly as you've told it to me, to Inspector Chatto, who's investigating.'

'Why should I?'

'I could give you a lot of reasons. In the first place it's your duty.'

'Hell. I told you I don't like the — police.'

'All right then. If that means nothing to you, let me tell you something else. How do you know you're not suspected of this murder?'

'Me? Why should I shoot that rat?'

'Why should anybody? You're known to have had a row with him, but no one knows how serious that row was. You admit you met him and a few minutes later you heard a shot. You had your gun with you. Altogether a nice little case could be made against you, Mr Bridge.'

The farmer was silent.

'Do *you* think I did it?' he asked suddenly, rather ingenuously.

'I'm not saying whether I do or whether I don't. But I *do* say that you've given me some evidence which the police may think important. There's no doubt at all you should see them.'

'I suppose I shall have to.'

'And tell them the truth,' added Beef, nodding significantly.

I was surprised to see that the aggressive Mr Bridge took this quite calmly. He stood up and after the briefest good night lurched out.

'What do you think of *that*?' I asked Beef.

I might have known that he would grow mysterious.

'Interesting,' was all he said.

'Do you think he was speaking the truth?'

'Some of it, anyway. If not all.'

'Then who was the man in the raincoat?' I asked sceptically.

Beef looked at me almost as though he presumed to think me foolish.

'Flipp, of course,' he said.

'I'm glad you know who it was,' I rejoined. 'Perhaps you know the murderer as well?'

'Got a pretty good idea,' admitted Beef. Then raising his voice he called to Mr Bristling, who was still wiping glasses in the bar, having a distaste, as he often said, for going to bed before he'd 'got straight'.

'Is there a Boy Scout troop here?' was Beef's surprising question to the publican.

'There certainly is. Very keen they are. Mr Packham runs it.'

'What on earth?' I asked Beef. Privately I sometimes think he is little more than an overgrown Boy Scout himself.

'Handy sometimes, Scouts,' he said. 'I think I can give them a little job that will please them *and* be useful. I must see that curate to-morrow. Then, of course, we must call on Aston, the solicitor.'

'I don't see why.'

'Red tape,' explained Beef, and with a huge ill-mannered yawn took himself off to bed.

CHAPTER EIGHTEEN

A Lawyer and Some Boy Scouts

AT breakfast next morning I told Beef that I thought things were going very slowly. He seemed to take pleasure in stumping steadily through a case, instead of showing flashes of brilliance like his more famous confrères. I wanted action.

'You're going to have it to-day,' he said. 'We're going on the bus to Ashley.'

'I mean real action.'

'What, another murder? Or a chase across the country of someone who turns out to have nothing to do with the case?'

'Well, *action*,' I returned.

'All in good time,' chuckled Beef. 'You wait till we get these Boy Scouts on the job. You'll have action all right then.'

We waited outside the Post Office for the green single-decker bus which would take us into Ashley, and Beef seemed to enjoy being stared at by the small boys who knew him to be a detective. When the bus drew up he took an awkward little seat beside the driver who also sold the tickets. I could see that he meant to get into conversation with him. But he might have used a little more originality in his approach.

'Nice day,' he commented gruffly.

'Cold,' said the driver.

'How long does it take into Ashley?'

'About half an hour.'

'How many of you are there on this run?'

The driver did not seem to resent this clumsy catechism.

'Only the two. Me and George Rivers.'

'Did you take her in on Christmas Eve?'

'Yes.'

'Happen to notice who was on her on the seven o'clock run?'

'Not many. They'd finished their shopping by then. Three or four, I think.'

Beef leaned very close to the man and tried to make his voice inaudible to the rest of us.

'See. I'm on this murder case,' he said.

'I know you are.'

'And there's a bit of information I'd like from you.'

'You're welcome.'

'Do you happen to remember whether Mrs Pluck, the housekeeper of the old gentleman who lives by the wood, was on that bus?'

The driver whistled.

'So that's it, is it? It was her done him in, eh? Well, she looks as though she could of.'

'Now don't be running away with any silly ideas,' said Beef severely. 'I never said nothing about her doing anyone in. I just wanted to know if she was on the bus on Christmas Eve.'

'Well, she wasn't.'

'Quite sure?'

'Quite. I'd of noticed. Well, you couldn't miss her, could you?'

Beef laughed.

'Bit of a fright, isn't she? But don't you go talking to people as though I suspected her, see? Never do. I should have a case for slander on my hands before you could say knife.'

'That's all right,' said the driver, and they began to talk of other matters.

When we arrived in Ashley, Beef inquired the way to the office of Mr Aston, the solicitor, and we found it near the market place. Mr Aston had not come in yet, his clerk said, and without being invited to do so Beef sat down in the outer office to wait. The clerk, a dim and pinched-looking man of middle age, busied himself with the morning's mail.

Again Beef started with elephantine awkwardness to try

making conversation. But he got only a brief nod to his comments on the weather, the food shortage, and the price of liquor.

Presently, however, he got his chance. The clerk was tying up a bundle of papers.

'Is that what you call red tape?' Beef asked.

The clerk looked up as though for the first time Beef had touched on something which could interest him.

'It is.'

'But it's not red at all. It's pink.'

A faint smile crossed the clerk's face.

'That was precisely the comment of a gentleman sitting here a few weeks ago. "It's not red," he said, "it's pink."'

'Ah,' said Beef. 'Great minds think alike. Who was the other one to remark on it?'

'One of our clients. A Mr Chickle, from Barnford. He seemed *most* interested in the subject. He even asked, if I remember rightly, how it was sold, and I told him in spools.'

'Well now,' cried Beef. 'That *is* funny! Because I was just going to ask you myself. What do they look like?'

The clerk pulled open a drawer in which we could see a number of spools of the pink tape and handed one to Beef, who solemnly examined it.

'Mind if I keep this?' he asked. 'I want it for a bit of a lark. Red tape, you know!'

'It's not easy to get,' said the clerk dubiously.

'You got plenty.'

'Oh, very well,' said the clerk rather sulkily, and turned with marked concentration to his work.

Soon after that a buzzer sounded and we were shown in to Mr Aston.

The solicitor was a grey and portly man with horn-rimmed glasses and a very smart suit. He affected, I thought, to be busier than he was, and quickly asked what he could do for us.

'It's about this murder,' said Beef.

'Shoulter?'

'Ah.'

'I know nothing about it.'

'You have a client called Wellington Chickle, I believe?' said Beef solemnly.

'I have. At least I have undertaken one matter for Mr Chickle.'

'And the nature of that matter?' asked Beef.

The solicitor stared at him.

'On what possible grounds do you put such a question?'

'Investigating. Representing the dead man's sister.'

'Am I expected to see some connexion between that and my client?'

'Just wanted to know what he came to see you about,' said Beef, rather abashed.

'Then I'm afraid your curiosity – I can scarcely call it any-thing else – will remain unsatisfied. Mr Chickle's business was confidential.'

'I see. And where were you that afternoon?'

The solicitor looked up sharply.

'I don't think I can have heard you correctly,' he said.

'You heard. I asked where you was on the afternoon when Shoulter was murdered. You live out that way, I believe.'

Mr Aston pressed his buzzer and his clerk appeared.

'Show these men out and don't admit them again,' he snapped.

I wondered whether to attempt some kind of explanation or apology for Beef's gross blunder. But he was signing to me from the door and I followed him from the room in con-fusion. To my annoyance Beef had no sooner reached the street than he started laughing.

'What on earth made you put that idiotic question?' I de-manded.

'I thought you'd like another suspect,' grinned Beef. I did not reply.

Back in Barnford we went at about four o'clock to the house of Mr and Miss Packham. They received us in a friendly manner, which did not seem to chill even when Beef began by saying that he had come to ask a favour.

'We're used to that,' said the curate. 'What is it this time?'

'I understand you run a troop of Boy Scouts?'

'I do.'

'I was wondering if they could do a little job for me. Sort of good deed, you know.'

'What sort of job?'

'Well. I want them to search a certain area.'

'Footprints?'

'No. Not footprints. If you would not mind I would explain to them myself what I want. How would that be?'

Mr Packham considered.

'Nothing against the Law, I take it?'

'Oh, no. They would be helping the Law.'

'No danger? None of your murderers about?'

'No danger,' promised Beef.

'Then I don't see why not. It's a Scout Night to-night. You could come along to the Lady Flitch Hall and explain just what you want.'

Suddenly both brother and sister assumed an attitude of attentive listening. They were quite motionless, staring before them. I tried to speak, but received a vicious 'Sshh!' from Miss Packham.

'What is it?' Beef inquired.

'Tea!' shouted the curate's sister. 'I heard the rattle of cups!'

'Stay and have some?' said the curate very tentatively.

'I think we'll go back to our own place,' said Beef with unusual tact. 'They'll be expecting us. See you at the Hall at – what time?'

'Six. Six.' Mr Packham's manner had become absent.

At six o'clock, therefore, I accompanied Beef to the hall, and we found ourselves surrounded as we entered by countless small boys, some of them wearing the uniform of Scouts. I felt very self-conscious, for I knew that on such occasions Beef was apt to pose a good deal, and to talk to the boys as benevolent schoolmasters or cheerful uncles talked in the boys' stories of half a century ago. This is not well received by modern boys who expect a man-to-man form of address.

As we entered we found that Mr Packham was deeply engaged with a few youngsters who seemed to know the way to his heart. One had brought him half a dozen eggs and another a pair of stored apples with skins wrinkled from a stay in some straw-covered loft. There were two other packages the precise contents of which were not apparent though guessable.

'Splendid. Splendid,' he was saying. 'Good chaps. Most grateful. My sister *will* appreciate these. Hullo, here's Sergeant Beef.'

There was a good deal of fuss and movement in the hall before the boys could be got into the chairs facing the platform, but it was achieved eventually, and Mr Packham rose to lecture them. He explained that they were going to be addressed by a real London detective, a description at which I shivered. Indeed, the whole proceedings seemed to me silly in the extreme. Whatever Beef wanted, I could not see that a lot of little boys running about thinking that they were sleuths would help much, and I was frankly nervous when I thought how Beef would address them. My worst fears were realized. When Mr Packham had finished he stood up and sticking his thumbs in the arm-holes of his waistcoat turned to the troop.

'Boys,' he said. 'Would you like to help me catch a murderer?'

He pronounced the word as though he were a comedian giving an imitation of an old-fashioned melodrama, dragging out the first syllable through a series of vowels. To my surprise there was a murmur of eager assent.

'If you'll do what I ask you,' he went on, 'you may be the means of bringing him to the gallows. All I need now is a little more evidence and you can help me get it.'

This clumsy approach seemed to appeal to the boys, who looked keen and eager.

'I want you to comb Deadman's Wood,' said Beef. 'Every inch of it.'

He paused for effect.

'Split up into parties,' he said. 'Organize yourselves. See that not a little piece of ground escapes you. And pick up anything you find. It's no good looking for footprints. They've all gone by now. But anything else. Anything else at all you may find you bring to this hall to-morrow night. Got the idea?'

They had. There was a rustle and chatter of expectation.

'And there's something else,' Beef continued. 'I want you to look at the barks of the trees all round that bungalow where Mr Chickle lives. Say up to twenty yards from there. See if you can find one that's split about a bit. You might. I don't say you will. But you might. The boy who finds that gets a reward. And one for any boy who finds anything in the wood that'll help me with my investigations. Now are there any questions you would like to ask?'

One boy wanted to know what they were to look for in particular.

'Ah,' said Beef. 'I can't tell you that for the very good reason that I don't know myself. You just keep your eyes skinned.'

'Who did it?' asked a thin boy with glasses.

'That's what you're going to help to find out,' returned Beef. 'Now off you go and divide it all up into squares. And plan out how you set about it. We'll meet here to-morrow night. All right?'

There was a shout of excitement as the meeting broke up.

CHAPTER NINETEEN

Night in Deadman's Wood

'Got a torch?' asked Beef after our meal that evening.

'Yes.'

'And some nice warm clothes?'

'I've got a greatcoat. Why?'

'We may be out all night.'

'What on earth for?'

'You wanted action, didn't you?'

'Yes, but I don't want to fool about all night for nothing.'

'I don't think it will be for nothing. Now look here – this case is more interesting than you think. It's a nasty business and we're going to find out the truth. It's all very well for you to think of it as nothing but a story – I tell you that there has been some clever and some dirty thinking done and, after all, a pretty violent crime. What we see to-night, if it happens as I think it will, is going to bring us a lot nearer the truth. And I'm serious about it.'

'That's fine. By the way you've been clowning about with Boy Scouts –'

'Those kids are going to be useful – even if they find nothing, as I think you'll see presently.'

'Well, since you won't even tell me whom you suspect I can only take your word for that.'

'It's not as easy as just suspecting someone. There are several people involved in this business – some of them innocent, perhaps. And as to suspecting, you know everything I know, so your suspicions are as good as mine. Well, I've never let you down yet, have I? You come along with me to-night and you may see something.'

'Very well. Where are we going?'

'To call on Mr Chickle, of course.'

I let the 'of course' pass, and prepared to follow Beef, accepting his suggestion of warm clothes and a torch. He himself had a woollen scarf round his neck when we set out. It was a dark night with a thin chilly drizzle from low clouds. We needed our torches to find the footpath across to Mr Chickle's house. I trudged along, taking care not to slip on the sticky ground and not attempting to get more information from Beef, since I know from experience that it is useless to catechize him.

We found 'Labour's End' to be well lighted, and I was glad of its cheerful aspect as we approached. But I thought there was something sinister about the gaunt figure of Mrs Pluck when she opened the door to us. She stared at us without speaking, and I'm sure there was fear in her big, hollow eyes. I had the impression that she found our visit unwelcome, though half-expected, and that she was relieved when Beef asked to see Mr Chickle.

The old gentleman was sitting beside a large fire when we entered his cosy book-lined room, and rose to greet us. In his manner, too, I sensed something strange, though with him it certainly was not fear.

Beef spoke as respectfully and politely as I could wish. He called Mr Chickle 'Sir', and said that he had come to warn him that his peace would probably be disturbed on the following day by an invasion from Boy Scouts.

Mr Chickle beamed and assured Beef that so far from disturbing him it would be a pleasure. As he grew older, he said, he liked more and more to see young people enjoying themselves, and it would not be the first time that the Scouts had played Cowboys and Indians in the wood.

'They won't be playing Cowboys and Indians this time,' said Beef rather harshly. 'They'll be doing a little job for me.'

Mr. Chickle seemed amused and mildly interested, and wondered if 'detectives and criminals' was a new variation of the game.

'In a way you might say so,' said Beef. 'What they're going to do is to search every inch of Deadman's Wood in parties. Every inch of it. And bring me whatever they find.'

'And what will they find?' asked Mr Chickle blandly.

'I shouldn't be surprised but what they might find something that will help to clear up this murder case.'

'Yes. I see. A clue, in fact?'

'Perhaps a clue.'

'It's very good of you to have come up to tell me,' smiled Mr Chickle.

'Well, we were on our way back from Copling, sir. I thought we would just call in.'

And Beef almost literally licked his chops just as a village policeman might when he has brought back a straying dog to his owner and expects to be offered a drink. Mr Chickle was not slow to perceive what Beef expected of him.

'A drink, Sergeant?' he suggested. 'I have a little reserve of Scotch, I'm glad to say.'

'I don't mind if I do, sir,' said Beef inevitably, and before long we were wishing good health to our host. But we did not linger for more than a few moments over the drink. Beef remembered that we had a darts match at our inn, and after cordial good nights we started towards Barnford.

But we had not gone more than fifteen yards when Beef stopped round the bend of a curve.

'Now,' he said, 'we go back and wait. If anyone comes out of the door of that house we follow him or her. But we don't get ourselves seen or heard until I speak out. Got it?'

It is at moments like this that Beef is at his best. In spite of his age and bulk – for he is close on fifty now and a heavy and powerful man at that – he can move as swiftly and silently as some great feline. He ceases to be the ungainly overgrown boy that I sometimes think him, and becomes genuinely a man of action. I am the first to criticize Beef, but I always admit that in an emergency his nerve and quickness of action are remarkable.

In the drizzle and darkness of that night he led the way to a point from which, while remaining concealed ourselves, we could watch both the front door and back door of 'Labour's End'. And there we stood, sheltered a little from the cold moisture of the night, but still wet, chilled, and uncomfortable for the best part of an hour. Beef discouraged me even from whispering, and when I signed to him that I would like to smoke a cigarette, he shook his head vigorously. I had begun to think that he had miscalculated and that our wet vigil was to be in vain, when some lights were switched out in the house, and a few moments later we saw the small figure of Mr Chickle in the open doorway outlined against the only light left burning within. He had opened the front door noiselessly and was engaged in closing it in silence.

'Ready?' whispered Beef.

When the little man started up the path which led to Miss Shoulter's home, we were behind him. I followed Beef as he dodged behind trees in his advance, keeping us out of sight and hearing, but never losing sight of Chickle. It was exhausting and difficult, but at least it was what I had demanded of Beef – it was action.

Presently Beef, who was ahead of me and could see our quarry, stopped. For some minutes I had been unable to catch more than a glimpse of Mr Chickle and had been satisfied to leave observation to Beef while I concentrated on moving in silence and remaining unseen. It appeared now that Beef was annoyed by something that had happened on the path ahead.

'He's dived into the wood,' he whispered to me. 'Can't follow him there. Just have to wait here and chance it.'

'Chance what?'

'You'll see.'

Again there was a long uncomfortable wait. My feet felt as though they had been pushed into a 'Frigidaire' for several hours, and I was longing for a smoke. Beef, however, seemed to strain his eyes in watching the path ahead, never moving from beside me and never turning away. Ten or fifteen minutes must have passed.

Suddenly, Beef began to walk forward, no longer dodging among the trees, and at the same time flashed his powerful torch far down the path ahead. In its beam I could see Mr Chickle coming towards us. Beef was talking loudly to me.

'We shall have to hurry,' I heard him say. 'Ah, here's Mr Chickle. Why, you've dropped your parcel, sir. There it is just in the grass behind you.'

'So I have,' said Mr Chickle.

Beef stooped to pick up the little bundle which had been dropped. It consisted of something wrapped in a piece of mackintosh. Beef handed it politely to Mr Chickle.

'Thanks, thanks. It really doesn't matter. Very much obliged to you.'

I had never seen the little man in such a state of confusion.

No one moved for a few moments. Then Mr Chickle seemed to pull himself together.

'Darts match cancelled?' he asked. There was nothing openly sarcastic in his tone, but I felt that it was not quite natural.

'Yes. The other side never turned up.' It was funny, I thought, that it was Beef who did the explaining of our presence there, and Chickle who said nothing to justify his.

'To tell you the truth, sir,' Beef went on. 'We have just heard a bit more from the police. We were on our way to call on Mr Bridge.'

Mr Chickle became animated.

'Mr Bridge, eh? I told you he was a violent young man.'

'Ah,' said Beef. 'You've been having a stroll yourself, sir?'

Mr Chickle seemed to be deciding whether or not he should speak.

'Yes, Sergeant. And to tell the truth, I've made a very curious discovery. I was going to keep it for the police, but since you've come along so opportunely, I may as well tell you first.'

'Very much obliged to you.'

Mr Chickle began to unroll the mackintosh of his parcel and revealed the largest pair of woman's shoes I have ever seen.

'Well, I never!' said Beef. 'Miss Shoulter's, I take it?'

'They *were* Miss Shoulter's,' said Mr Chickle, who seemed

now to have recovered himself. 'They were made especially for her. Outsize, you know. But they have been in my possession since then. I had to purchase them in a lot at one of our worthy curate's auctions. What I cannot understand is this. Two months ago I myself put these shoes in my own dustbin, expecting, I might say hoping, never to set eyes on them again. And to-night while I'm taking the little stroll I have for the sake of sound sleep, I find them wrapped in this piece of old mackintosh beside the footpath. How do you account for that?'

'Funny,' was Beef's comment.

'Do you think it has any connexion with the crime?'

'Hard to say,' said Beef. 'Very hard to say.'

A few minutes later we left him, this time to go home and sleep, I hoped. I know that when at last we reached our inn, having waited another half-hour in the cold and rain to make sure that we should not have another encounter with Chickle, I was pleased to get between the sheets. But Beef had been chuckling to himself with pleasure all the way home.

CHAPTER TWENTY

Boy Scouts at Work

AND what must Beef do next day but organize and lead his ridiculous Boy Scouts' treasure hunt. It was a Saturday, I remember, and having a holiday the boys turned up in great numbers. Beef sat under a tree with the patrol-leaders about him and intricate plans seemed to be drawn up during the discussion in the course of which there was a good deal of repetition of that 'every inch' phrase of Beef's which had already been used a number of times. Personally, I sat apart and smoked a pipe, regretting once again that I had relented in my decision to throw up the chronicling of Beef's exploits and turn to the less eccentric profession of insurance. Boy Scouts searching 'every inch' of a wood, I said. Ridiculous. A good detective should know exactly what to look for and exactly where it was likely to be found, not sit discussing plans of action with patrol-leaders or whatever these sniffing and coughing youngsters might be.

Last night's episode, I admitted, had been curious. If Beef was right in supposing that the footmarks of Miss Shoulter found near the corpse had been made by someone wearing her shoes, what in the world had little Mr Chickle been doing with them at eleven o'clock at night on the very foot-path of the crime? Why had he tried to drop them out of sight? Why had he said he had found them *on* the footpath when Beef had seen him disappear into the thickness of the wood and return with them? I flatter myself on being a pretty shrewd judge of a man's truthfulness, and I was convinced that his story of a little stroll for the sake of sleeping well was a fabrication. Moreover, Beef had actually been expecting him to do something of the sort that he did.

And yet I could not bring myself to suspect Mr Chickle. Apart from the fact that he had no motive, had never even met Shoulter so far as we knew, he was obviously incapable of murder. Or even if one's imagination could be stretched to a point of believing that he might have poisoned some-one, the mere association of a violent crime with the kindly little retired watchmaker was absurd.

Mrs Pluck, now, was a different matter. She had proved herself a liar in the most incriminating matter of her alibi on the night of the crime, and also in the scarcely less in-teresting one of her ability to fire a gun. She was a big mas-culine woman who could easily be capable of murder, I thought, when I remembered her big, horny hands and dour face. Then I had a brilliant inspiration. There was some mystery about her husband. I remembered her indignation when Beef had asked his name and her flat refusal to discuss that part of her life. There was also a story that Shoulter himself had been married and had deserted his wife. What if these two stories were one? What if Shoulter had been the absconding husband of Mr Chickle's strange housekeeper? Then with her false story of her movements on the night of the crime, the whole thing fitted. True the last shot noticed by the inhabitants of Deadman's Wood had been at half-past six. But what of that? With shooting so common in the vicinity, a report could easily have been unnoticed. Or per-haps Chickle knew the truth and to save his housekeeper was deliberately lying to us. That would account, too, for his evasions and odd behaviour. He knew, perhaps, that it was Mrs Pluck who had worn the outsize shoes and had con-cealed them in some place afterwards. When he had heard that the Scouts were to search the wood, he had decided to retrieve them in order to save the woman. It was all far more in conformity with the character of Chickle as I knew him than any suspicion that he himself was implicated.

But there were other suspects. My investigations into crime have taught me to avoid fixed ideas and to keep an absolutely open mind. There was Bridge, for instance. All very well to accept his story because he was the kind of man whom Beef liked – hard-drinking, hard-living, and over-masculine. Look at it how you like, he was a man who well might have committed a violent crime. And it was surely something of a coincidence that he had been near the scene of the crime within a few moments of the firing of the first double shot, and that by his own admission. I was by no means prepared to accept his story blindly, and what was more, I did not believe that Beef had done so.

Of course, I could name others who might be involved, and I had to admit that the case looked pretty black against Flipp, the police suspect. There was Miss Shoulter, who might also have had a motive for all we knew, and Mr Aston was a 'possible' since he lived in Copling, and could have been in Deadman's Wood that day, especially since it was red tape (of a kind which Beef had now found to be identical with that in his office) which had been used for faking the suicide.

'Going over your suspects?' enquired Beef suddenly.

I started. I had not noticed him approaching.

'Certainly not,' I said, rather huffed. 'I know who did it.'

Beef gave his coarse laugh.

'You know, do you?'

I decided to brazen it out.

'I do. And I shall be interested to see how long it takes you to work it out.'

'The police know, too,' reflected Beef.

'Oh, the police,' I said, rather contemptuously, I'm afraid.

'You don't want to underrate them. Chatto's a very shrewd chap.'

'Yes,' I said. 'But it will take more than shrewdness to solve this crime.' Once having taken up this rather confident line I had decided to go on speaking with authority. 'It will take a quality which I don't think that either of you have in sufficient strength – that is, imagination.'

Beef laughed again.

'Well, all I can say is if you know who did it you've got a wonderful imagination. Wonderful.'

'How are your search parties doing?' I asked in order to change the subject.

'They're on the job now. They'll cover every inch . . .'

'Exactly. Every inch of the wood. In the meantime what do we do?'

'Take it easy,' said Beef, 'and await developments.'

At that moment a dishevelled youth who needed a haircut *and* a pocket handkerchief sidled up. He was flushed with excitement, but he did not seem anxious to say anything in front of me.

'Well, Lionel?' asked Beef, for he had already learnt all the boys' names. 'Lionel's the leader of the Porcupine Patrol,' he explained to me.

' 'Ippopotamus,' corrected Lionel.

'Well, what is it?'

He glanced uneasily in my direction.

'That's all right,' said Beef grandly. 'This gentleman is in my confidence up to a point. You may speak in front of him.'

I ignored this ridiculous mummery.

'Found something,' said the boy called Lionel.

'What have you found?'

When at last he spoke it came out with a rush.

'You know you said we was to look at the barks of all them trees round that bungalow where that old toff lives with that old housekeeper down the bottom end of the path towards Barnford, don't you? Well, we done it.'

'What?'

'Looked. And just as you go into the wood, well about as far as a cricket pitch only perhaps a bit shorter, there's a tree where the bark's been ripped as you might say to ribbons just below a bough which runs out straight towards the bungalow, and Albert Stoke, whose father's a keeper over at Whitton, though he's laid up now, says a gun's been fired straight at the tree from quite near and you better come and have a look.'

Beef nodded.

'Yes, I did.'

'Did what?' I asked disgustedly.

'Did better go and have a look. Come on.'

We found the tree in question surrounded by eager youngsters. I wondered what Mr Chickle might think if he chanced to look from the window of his study, which directly overlooked us. I felt extremely foolish and Beef went through a lot of hocus-pocus with a tape measure while the Boy Scouts watched in breathless silence. The bough, as the boy had said, stretched out almost precisely at right angles to the tree and pointed straight towards Mr Chickle's home, as though the tree were a natural fingerpost. And there was a narrow, but unbroken, space from the tree to Mr Chickle's lawn.

Beef had examined the bark of the tree just below the junction with the bough, and had found it scarred and charred as Lionel had described. If it was the result of a gunshot the weapon must have been quite close to it, indeed one would have said along the under side of the bough itself. The same idea seemed to have occurred to Beef, for he was scanning the bough closely. Suddenly, to my disgust, he actually pulled a magnifying glass from his pocket, on which a chorus of 'Coo!' went up from the boys.

'Beef!' I expostulated.

'Come and look at this,' was his only reply, and he indicated some indentations and scratches on the bough. 'See?' And turning to the members of the Hippopotamus Patrol he declaimed, 'Boys, you've done it. This will be a great help. I'm proud of you. Now go on to your square of the wood. That's from the wire fence to where Nelson Grover found the jay's nest, isn't it?'

'That's right,' they chorused and sped away with their eyes on the ground.

We ourselves, I am thankful to say, returned to the village, but not before Beef had reminded his assistants that they were to meet in the hall that evening and that they were to bring all they had found.

We spent the afternoon quietly; at least I was quiet, but Beef had a sleep, which in the daytime and after his noon glass of beer is usually a thunderous process. At tea-time Miss Shoulter looked in to see how we were getting on. She seemed to have a childlike confidence in Beef and urged him not to spare time and expense in his investigations.

When it was time to go round to the Lady Flitch Hall I accompanied Beef, not without misgivings. To tell a score or more of vigorous youngsters to bring in everything they found in a wood seemed to me an incautious proceeding, and as we entered the place my worst fears were realized. I'm bound to admit that Beef did not delay in giving orders for the disposal of a dead and half-decomposed cat which was the most offensive of the articles collected, but it was long before its aftermath had left us, in spite of hastily opened windows. Four snares attributed to the possession of Old Fletcher who was known not to be above a bit of poaching were not, as they should have been, handed over to the police, and the whitened skull of a sheep was presented to the Mongoose Patrol as a souvenir. Three boots which might have been discarded by tramps in Queen Victoria's reign were consigned to the dustbin, and the remains of an umbrella likewise. A number of pieces of rusty metal were promised rather optimistically to salvage; and broken china was thrown out. An empty bottle was also said by Beef to be of no account, which led to some argument among the Water Buffaloes.

'Might of had poison in it, mightn't it?' one of them suggested, to be snubbed promptly by a Rattlesnake who reminded him that Shoulter had been shot.

At last Beef came to the scraps of paper which had been collected into one heap. After a moment he seized the freshest of these and calling me to the light showed it to me. I must say I was impressed, and I could see that Beef was as excited as one of the Boy Scouts. For it was an envelope addressed to Mr and Mrs Flipp and containing a Christmas card. Absently I examined its still vivid design – a steaming football of Christmas pudding with a sprig of holly in it. Inside were the printed words 'Good Cheer'! And under them were scrawled the names of the curate and his sister.

'Who found this?' asked Beef.

A bespectacled boy with thin legs was pushed forward.

'Where was it?'

'I've marked the spot, Sarge,' he returned cheekily. 'I'll take you there to-morrow. It was ten paces into the wood itself from the clearing where the body was found.'

Beef silently handed him his reward.

CHAPTER TWENTY-ONE

A Nice Young Couple

ONCE again Beef took his information to Chatto. I thought that this time there was something a trifle patronizing in the C.I.D. man's manner. Or if not patronizing, perhaps encouraging, as though he considered Beef a younger and less experienced man who must be kept going by kindness.

Without comment Beef described the marks on the tree near Mr Chickle's house and left the inspector to draw what conclusions he chose from them. Chatto scribbled a note but said nothing. When Beef referred to the evening on which we had watched Mr Chickle with the outsize shoes, Chatto nodded impatiently.

'Yes,' he said. 'Chickle has reported that and brought in his finds.'

'Good.'

Chatto showed some interest in Bridge's story, particularly his account of the man in the raincoat. It was agreed by all three of us that the man was Flipp, but the conclusions that each of us drew from the fact may have varied. In the matter of the red tape Chatto nodded. It was when Beef produced the Christmas card and described where it had been found that Chatto was really enlivened.

'That's about the last straw,' he said. 'I think we may as well arrest Flipp.'

'Think so?' said Beef. 'Of course you know your business best, but it looks a bit circumstantial to me. Nothing really to convince a jury with. And Flipp's not the man to plead guilty.'

Chatto looked mysterious.

'We've got something else,' he said quietly. 'The poison book. Hidden under the floorboards in Shoulter's room. Flipp bought the morphine all right. Signed for it under the name of Phelps two weeks before his wife died. Our hand-writing experts say there isn't a doubt of it.'

'Then why not arrest him for the murder of his wife? You seem to have a better case than what you've got here.'

Chatto shook his head.

'It needs the two cases,' he said. 'Much more convincing. But why do you want me to wait? Have you got another iron in the fire?'

'Not what you could call an iron. But I *should* like to know a little more about Mrs Pluck. She wasn't on the bus that Christmas Eve.'

'Oh, Mrs Pluck,' said Chatto in a voice which implied that he had no interest in the woman at all.

'Well, there are some rather queer things about Mrs Pluck,' apologized Beef.

'How long do you think it will take to clear them up?'

'Give me three days.'

Chatto thought for a minute.

'It's true that I would like to get something a bit more concrete before arresting Flipp. We've got motive, opportunity, and presence near the scene of the crime. But they don't constitute a final proof. I don't think we shall make an arrest before next week-end.'

'That's good,' said Beef. 'That'll give me time to clear up all my points. Chickle's going away for a few days to-morrow.'

'Yes,' said Chatto, as though anxious to show that he knew as much as or more than Beef about Chickle's movements. 'To stay with his old friend Flusting in South London. Neighbouring shopkeepers for twenty years, I understand.'

'Some Lodge,' said Beef. 'That'll give me a chance for a nice quiet chat with Mrs Pluck to-morrow.'

'You're welcome,' said Chatto.

But the 'nice quiet chat', as Beef had called it, turned out to be one of the most interesting conversations among the many in this loquacious case.

'Come in,' she said wearily, as though she had guessed

that sooner or later we should arrive at the door with the object of questioning her. 'What is it this time?'

Beef slowly lowered himself into a chair.

'How's Mr Chickle?'

She looked up suspiciously.

'Why?'

Beef gave a ponderous shrug of his shoulders.

'Just wondered.'

'Well, if you want to know, he's been funny. Very funny.'

This common, but curious, misuse of the language did not seem to perturb Beef.

'In what way?' he asked.

'Ever since it happened, he won't hardly speak. He's all right with you, I dare say, but it's my belief he puts that on. He used to be nice and chatty and always have a civil word when he met me. Now he looks as though he's seen a ghost half the time. Proper miserable. And he's off his food.'

'Worrying?'

'Well, not so much worrying as miserable. Anybody'd think he'd lost all his money. I can't make it out at all. It's something to do with the murder, because up to that afternoon he was right as a trivet. Used to laugh to himself. Thought himself someone, too. D'you know one day after he'd been sitting in his room writing, he turned round to me and said – "I'm a remarkable man, Mrs Pluck." "Are you, sir?" I said. Well, I mean, what could you say? "Yes," he says, "and what's more," he says, "the time will come when everyone'll recognize it." "Indeed, sir?" "Yes," he says, "long after my death, of course." And he laughs away to himself as though he was pleased as Punch. But he's not been like that since the murder, I can tell you.'

'Ah,' put in Beef encouragingly. Then, since Mrs Pluck volunteered no more information, he added: 'Did you ever see that big pair of lady's shoes he had?'

She gave a croak of laughter.

'Did I not? He had them brought home with a lot of old shoes he bought at the jumble sale. Nothing any good except a pair of carpet slippers he took to and wore every night. When I first saw them I asked him whatever sort of an elephant they were made for, but he didn't say a word, and I dare say that was because they'd belonged to Miss Shoulter and I've always fancied he was a bit sweet on her. Well, they were lying about for weeks, then I never saw them again till a few nights ago when he brought them home wrapped up in an old bit of mackintosh after I'd gone to bed one evening. Well, it was the night you came to see him last. Next morning he saw me looking at them and spoke very sharp. "Don't touch those!" he said. "They're for the police." And that was all.'

Beef spoke as sharply as Chickle must have done.

'Did you ever wear them?'

'Wear them? Me? I'd have been lost in them.'

'Did you even try them on?'

'No. I did not.'

'I see. Now there's something I'm going to ask you straight and I want a straight answer. What did you do on Christmas Eve?'

'I told you —'

'You told me you took the bus to Ashley and you never did nothing of the sort. I want to know where you were.'

Mrs Pluck's long lips remained pressed close together.

'Come on, now. Better speak straight out. We shall get to know sooner or later.'

'It wasn't anything special. If you must know I met my daughter.'

'Where?'

'Well, we had nowhere to go for a chat. I'd written to her to come over and meet me at the bus stop. Then we went round to the house of a lady who's a friend of mine. I suppose you'll want to know who she was, so I may as well tell you. It was Mrs Wilks, and we sat in her back room for an hour.'

'You must have wanted to see her urgent,' commented Beef.

'Not extra. Only it was Christmas Eve and anyone likes to see her own daughter then, don't they?'

'What did you talk about?'

'Family business.'

'Was Mrs Wilks there?'

'No. She left us together. Well, it was private.'

'What time were you there till?'

'Last bus for Ashley.'

'You went straight from that house to the bus station?'

'Yes.'

'And came straight home?'

'Yes.'

'Never went up the path at all?'

'Certainly not. And just as well I didn't with a dead corpse lying there all the time.'

'Did you have anything to say to your daughter about your husband?'

'My husband? I told you he left me nearly twenty years ago.'

'You told me a lot of things. And some of them were lies.'

'My daughter thinks he's dead.'

'And is he?'

'I don't know and I don't care.'

Mrs Pluck was breathing heavily. I thought that my theory was being confirmed.

'Where did you say you married him?'

'I didn't say and I'm not going to say. It's my affair and no one else's. I don't know why you want to keep on at me about things that are nothing to do with you. You're supposed to be finding out who murdered Shoulter.'

'And that,' said Beef triumphantly, 'is exactly what I am doing.'

'Not by asking me questions, you're not. I had nothing to do with it.'

'What's your daughter's address?'

'Never you mind.'

'That's silly, Mrs Pluck. We can find out easily enough.'

'You find out then. Only don't you start dragging her into this else you'll have her husband after you and he was a sergeant-major in the Commandos.'

'Have to chance that,' said Beef. 'So you won't tell me straight instead of having a lot of police inquiries made round her home?'

'The police would never do such a thing. Besides, Mr Chickle says it's Flipp they suspect and may arrest any minute. *They* won't pester me or her with a lot of silly questions.'

Beef stood up.

'Well, if you won't tell me you won't. But it won't take me long to find out.'

As we were walking home I asked him whether that wasn't rather an idle boast and pressed him to tell me how in fact he meant to discover it.

'Easy. We'll go and see Mrs Wilks now. Ten to one she's never thought to warn her.'

It took us some minutes after returning to Barnford to find out which was Mrs Wilks's cottage, but when we knocked on its door it was opened by a little, neat, smiling woman whom I mentally described as a nice old body.

'Excuse me,' said Beef amiably. 'Is Mrs Pluck's daughter here?'

'Mrs Muckroyd? Not to-night. She'll be over in a day or two, I expect. She always looks in here when she comes to see her Ma. Was it urgent?'

'Not extra. I shall be over her way to-morrow, so I can see her then. I can get there by bus, can't I?'

Mrs Wilks smiled cheerfully and I felt rather ashamed to take advantage of her trusting good nature.

'Yes. Change at Ashley. You'll find her home right in the village of Pitley. Get down at the post office. It's nothing wrong, I hope?'

'Nothing at all. I'm a friend of Mrs Pluck's, see? Have you known her long?'

'Only since she came here. Must be eight or nine months.'

'Well, I'm much obliged to you. I'll say good night.'

As we returned to the Crown, Beef chuckled.

'There you are. Told you it would be easy. Now it's time for a drop of pig's ear.'

'It always is,' I said bitterly.

'You're right there,' Beef retorted.

CHAPTER TWENTY-TWO

Mrs Pluck's Past

'ANYBODY would think we were commercial travellers or employed on finding out people's opinions for a Gallup Poll,' I said next day as we reached the village of Pitley. 'We seem to do nothing but knock on people's doors and ask questions.'

'We've got to find out the truth,' said Beef. 'People won't tell you things unless you ask. Besides, you ought to be pleased with this one. It's the first young lady we've had in this case.'

'Young married woman,' I pointed out.

'And that takes away all the glamour, does it?'

But I must say it didn't. When Mrs Muckroyd opened the door to us I caught my breath and wondered how she could be the daughter of the grim Mrs Pluck. She looked only about nineteen and was, if I may use the word, dainty in the extreme. The pale winter sun caught her fair hair and her eyes were blue and gay. She was smiling and would I think have been friendly and pleasant if Beef had not put his foot in it and announced in his coarse and brutal way that he had 'come about the murder'.

Her face changed in a moment. She looked startled, as well she might.

'What?' she cried.

'The murder over at Barnford.'

Her reaction this time was instantaneous.

'Jim!' she called.

Jim Muckroyd who emerged from an inner room was six foot four of solid Yorkshire manhood. I could well believe he had been a sergeant-major in the Commandos.

'What is it?' he asked.

'They . . . you tell him . . .' she gasped to Beef.

Beef stood his ground.

'Morning, Sergeant-major,' he said. 'I'm investigating the death of a man named Shoulter over at Barnford, and there's a little information Mrs Muckroyd could help us with.'

I think all of us became aware at this point that a head was over the garden wall to our left and the door to our right had opened suspiciously.

'Better come in,' said Jim Muckroyd, and we trooped into a warm little kitchen. On the table were the remains of the young couple's midday meal. There was a chair for each of us. Beef began talking.

'Thought I'd better tell you straight out what we wanted. No good pretending that we'd come to sell something and get into conversation that way. It's like this. I'm not the police. I've retired from that. Private investigator, see? Working for Miss Shoulter. And trying to find out who killed her brother.'

'What can we tell you?' asked Jim Muckroyd. 'I wasn't even here. Only got released three days ago.'

'Ah. But you see Mrs Muckroyd was over there that night. Seeing her mother.'

'That's right,' said the girl, who seemed to have recovered. 'Mum wrote to me to come over. She wanted to see me particular.'

'What time did you meet her?'

'About seven.'

'Half a minute,' said Muckroyd. 'Let's get this straight. Is my wife's mother suspected of having anything to do with this murder?'

Beef coughed.

'Well, it's like this,' he said. 'Mrs Pluck can't make up her mind to speak out straight. I won't say she's suspected and I won't say she's not. But when anyone won't talk out, and tells you things that turn out not to be true, you've got to follow up and find out the real facts. The best service you can do her is to tell me the gospel.'

Jim Muckroyd and Beef stared at one another for a few moments, then the Yorkshireman seemed to make up his mind to trust Beef.

'Tell him what you know, lass,' he said shortly to his wife.

'But I don't know anything! And you ought to be ashamed of yourself thinking bad about my mother. She's one of the best. What she's done for me you'd not believe – bringing me up and everything. And she's so kind-hearted she wouldn't hurt a fly, I *know* she couldn't have had anything to do with it.'

'Then if you'll speak out we'll soon get her clear. Now what was this urgent business she wanted to see you about on Christmas Eve?'

The girl's voice was so low that I scarcely caught her words.

'It was money,' she said. 'She needed some money.'

'Ah. Were you surprised? Or has she ever wanted money before?'

'Never. I was terribly surprised. Mum doesn't drink and doesn't spend anything on herself. And she's got a good job. She wouldn't tell me what it was for, either. I could see she was ever so worried. I asked her if she'd been gambling, and she said of course not. I couldn't get the truth out of her. It was something she didn't mean me to know. All she'd say was that it was for the sake of my happiness and she had to have ten pounds at once.'

'And did you give it to her?'

'Not at once. Jim was still away. I had to draw it out of the Post Office, but I sent it over a few days later. Then a funny thing happened. It came back by return of post. She said she did not need it now. Things had changed.'

'She seemed worried that night?'

'Ever so worried. Not herself a bit. I could see something was wrong.'

'What sort of thing?'

'Something big. Mum isn't one to get worried. I'd never seen her like that before.'

'Anything to do with her job?'

'I don't think so. She seemed to like that all right. She laughed a bit about the old fellow she worked for. But he treated her all right and she never said a word against him. No, it was something else, I think. She's had a hard life, you know. Father dying when I was a baby and that.'

'Do you happen to know, Mrs Muckroyd, where your mother met your father and where they were married?'

Mrs Muckroyd seemed surprised.

'Why, at her home at Pittenden, I suppose. Mum's father was a farmer there. I always understood from her that she'd married while she was still at home. Why?'

'Because I think I can find out what was on your mother's mind. Now you say you met her at seven?'

'Yes. She was standing waiting outside the post office when the bus came in. We went round to Mrs Wilks's and sat there talking. Then I left her to catch the last bus at ten o'clock.'

'Other times you've met her lately she's seemed herself, has she?'

'Well ... yes. But soon after she started to work for this Mr Chickle there was something that upset her. Then she seemed to get over that. I wish you *could* find out what it's all about.'

I did not speak, but I thought I knew. When she had taken the job at 'Labour's End' she had heard the name Shoulter as one of Mr Chickle's neighbours, and then she had learnt that Miss Shoulter had a ne'er-do-well brother and realized that it was none other than the husband who had deserted her many years before. But her state of mind on Christmas Eve had been caused by the fact that Shoulter had found her out and was demanding money, threatening to go over and see her daughter and tell her who he was if Mrs Pluck did not give him what he asked. The woman obviously loved her daughter and would do anything to shield her. The question was, had she gone to the length of murder? No one knowing Mrs Pluck could doubt that she was capable of it. I looked at the pretty, rather distressed girl and hoped that this would turn out not to be the truth.

Suddenly, as we sat there, the front door could be heard opening and in a moment the kitchen door too. Mrs Pluck was standing there, a really horrified expression on her gaunt face.

'Oh! They've got here! You haven't told them anything, Mabs?'

'Why, Mum, whatever's the matter?' cried Mrs Muckroyd, running to her.

Mrs Pluck was sobbing.

'I *knew* they'd come and question you. I *knew* they would. What have you told them?'

'Why, nothing, Mum. There was nothing *to* tell. Only about my meeting you that night and your being worried lately.'

Jim Muckroyd told her to sit down.

'Far best speak out,' he said. 'You've got nowt to hide.'

'You don't know. You don't understand.' She turned to Beef. 'I *told* you I never had anything to do with the murder. It was as much a shock to me as anyone. Why can't you leave us alone?'

'You place us in an embarrassing situation, Mrs Pluck,' I volunteered, since I could see that the situation was one which called for tact. 'It is our business to find out the whole truth of this. You did mislead us at first.'

'Only because I didn't tell you I'd met Mabel that night. I didn't want her dragged into it.'

'Still, you will admit that it was most misleading. Sergeant Beef and I have had to go to a great deal of trouble to find out the truth. And even now you won't tell us what is worrying you.'

'I haven't said anything's worrying me, have I?'

'You know there is something,' put in her daughter.

Mrs Pluck put away her handkerchief and turned with an angry look to Beef.

'I'll tell you what *is* worrying me,' she said. 'All this nosing and prying into the private business of folks that is nothing to do with anyone except themselves. Call yourself a detective and go and tell poor Emma Wilks you're a friend of mine to get Mabel's address then come over here startling the life out of her about a murder she doesn't know anything about. It's right down mean and cunning, and if there's any way I can have the Law on you I will.'

Beef looked rather sheepish, but help came from an unexpected quarter. Jim Muckroyd seemed to have the old-fashioned notion that men should stand together under feminine assault and had sensed that Beef meant no harm to him or his wife. He rallied with a quiet interpolation.

'Take it easy, ma,' he said. 'They've got their job to do like everyone else, and you did lead 'em up the garden. Now what is it you want to know from her?'

There was a very tense silence.

'I want to know the name of her first husband,' announced Beef solemnly.

Jim Muckroyd blinked.

'And you'll go so far as to say that the name of my mother-in-law's first husband has something to do with finding out who did this murder?'

'Sergeant Beef never asks questions out of mere curiosity,' I put in loyally.

'I'll go so far as to say that it might have,' said Beef.

'All right then. What was it, ma?'

'I've told him once,' Mrs Pluck retorted sulkily. 'I've only been married once. His name was Pluck.'

Beef stood up, and I followed his example. Jim Muckroyd came out with us, shutting the kitchen door behind him. When we reached the road he gave us a slow smile.

'The old girl's all right,' he said. 'I know her. She's been too wrapped up in the wife.'

'I can see that,' said Beef, and becoming more human added: 'And nobody can't blame her. You're a lucky man, Sergeant-major.'

'Dare say I am. I'd like to know that this business was cleared up though. Not a good thing having your mother-in-law questioned about a murder. When do you think you'll know the truth?'

'You may not like the truth,' said Beef.

'You don't think the old lady did it, do you?

'I didn't say that, did I? There's a lot of things I've got to find out before I say who did it. But when you start what she calls nosing and prying you sometimes have to find out things that are best forgotten, see? Still, if anything should come up which won't be very pleasant for you to hear, I don't think it would make much difference to you and your young missus, would it?'

Jim Muckroyd smiled.

'No,' he said. 'There's nothing could do that. Still, I'd like to know the old girl's out of it. She's a good sort.'

We all shook hands and Beef seemed relieved as Jim Muckroyd returned to his house.

'Nice young couple, that,' he announced. 'It's a good thing we meet some decent folk now and again in these cases. We see plenty of the other sort.'

I heartily agreed.

CHAPTER TWENTY-THREE

The Marriage Register

I ASKED Beef what he thought he had gained by the interview, and he said genially that he had got the one piece of information he required.

'To-morrow,' he added, 'we go to Pittenden.'

So that was it. Beef had hit on my idea and was going to get confirmation of the fact that Shoulter was Mrs Pluck's first husband. I smiled to myself to think that I had forestalled him, but said nothing except that I would accompany him next day.

We had to go on a slow local train and did not reach Pittenden, a small country town, until about noon. Beef thereupon announced that we should make for the Coach and Horses.

'Couldn't we just for once keep out of pubs?' I suggested coldly. 'I really get *rather* tired of this perpetual beer-swilling.'

'You can have cider then,' said Beef. 'Where else do you think we can go to find out what we want? There's only two places for gossip – the pub and the church. And we've had enough of parsons for this case.'

We entered the public bar and took our seats quietly at a deal table next to an elderly man who eyed us curiously. Beef wasted no time. If there is one thing in which he is expert it is turning the conversation in a bar to the matter that interests him most.

'Cold,' was his opening.

'Bitter,' returned the old man, referring to the weather and not to his drink.

'Been a hard winter,' continued Beef, who knew the dangers of impatience.

'It has. You come a long way?'

'London,' said Beef.

'Business?'

'In a way.'

'What line?'

'I'm not a traveller,' replied Beef. 'Family business.'

It was clear that the man's curiosity was aroused.

'Pittenden family?' he asked after a pause.

'It was,' said Beef. 'Before your time, I expect.'

The man smiled at that.

'Before *my* time, eh? Must be a hell of a long way back then. I was born here and so was my father and grandfather. Don't know any further back than that.'

'Ah,' said Beef, and drank his beer, leaving the next attack to the stranger.

'Were you born in Pittenden?' the latter asked.

'No. Londoner.'

'Relations this way perhaps?'

'Supposed to of. But I don't rightly know the name. I've heard they've died out now. Farmers.'

'Farmers, were they?'

'That's what I've heard. There was a woman of about my age was the daughter.'

Beef's manner suggested that every scrap of information was being dragged from him against his will, and this simple strategy seemed to inspire the stranger into efforts of concentration and memory.

'Know anything about them?'

'This woman I was speaking of got married down here. Matter of about twenty years ago. Had a little girl, too. But the fellow was no good and left her.'

'Twenty years ago?'

' 'Bout that.'

'I don't know who that could have been.'

'Farmers,' prompted Beef. 'Not so long after the last war.'

'Only daughter, was she?'

'Couldn't say,' said Beef, and appeared to have dismissed the matter from his mind as he rose to order three more drinks.

'Funny I can't think of that,' said the stranger.

'Thought it might be before your time,' mumbled Beef almost rudely. Then he turned to me and began a ridiculous conversation about the oil-painting on the wall, a subject on which he is particularly ignorant.

Suddenly there was a cry from the other man.

'I've got it,' he said. 'Old Will Thorogood's daughter. Married a London chap who went off and left her.'

'Thorogood, eh?'

'Yes. Used to have Rossback Farm. She was his only daughter, too. This chap came down here travelling in patent medicines, I believe. I can't remember his name. Fell in with old Thorogood's daughter and married her a month later. Everyone was surprised at the time because she was no beauty and no longer a girl.'

'What did she look like?' asked Beef.

The other laughed.

'More like a man than a woman, she was. Well, she'd worked on a farm since she was a kid. They say she could plough a field with anyone, but I don't know if that's true. I tell you what she was though – a wonderful housekeeper for the old man. Looked after him like a mother. That's why the old fellow didn't like it when she married this London chap.

'But that didn't last long. Soon as the baby was born he went off and left her, and she went back to her father. The old man wasn't doing too well – it was a bad time for small farms – and he was glad to have her. Then a couple of years later he died and Rossback Farm had to be sold up. There wasn't much left for this daughter we were speaking of and she went off into service somewhere and took the little girl with her. I never heard of her again.'

'Who was *her* mother then?' asked Beef idly.

'Old Thorogood married one of the Plucks from Leckley way. But she died before all this happened.'

Neither of us turned a hair at the mention of the name for which we had been listening. I saw my little theory being confirmed at every step. After Shoulter had left her and her father had died she had chosen her mother's maiden name under which to make a new start.

'D'you happen to remember where they were married?' persisted Beef. 'I mean this London chap and Miss Thorogood that was?'

'Yes. Parish church. I remember the wedding. Well, there's a good many that would. She looked a bit out of place in a wedding dress. Proper farm girl, *she* was.'

As artfully as Beef had turned the conversation in this direction he now diverted it to other matters. And a few minutes later we went through into a gloomy apartment which had 'Commercial Room' on the door and sat down to lunch.

'Means another parson, after all,' said Beef. 'We shall have to go and look at the register.'

I sighed. But it was obvious within a few moments of meeting Prebendary Boxe, the Rector of Pittenden, that he was not going to provide me with a touch of minor characterization, comic or otherwise. He was a keen-faced businesslike man who asked what he could do for us in a tone that implied that whatever it was he had not time to do it. Beef haltingly asked if he might refer to the register, and almost before he had finished speaking the rector nodded.

'My gardener will take you down. He's my verger as well, and has the keys. You may make a small contribution to the Church Expenses Fund to repay his trouble. You'll find the box in the south transept. Good afternoon.'

It took us half an hour to find what we wanted, for in the years following the last war the marriage and giving in marriage in Pittenden seemed to have been considerable. When at last we came on the entry we sought I could not repress a cry of triumph. For it was quite clear that the man who had married Hester Thorogood had been none other than Ronald Shoulter.

When he had returned the register to the locked cupboard the verger-gardener asked Beef whether the rector had told him to put a contribution in the Church Expenses box.

'You can give it to me,' he pointed out. 'I'll pop it in. Save you time.'

Beef complied and we left him to lock up.

As we returned to the station I informed Beef that this had been my theory from the first. I told him I had suspected the truth from the first minute that I had heard that Mrs Pluck had been deserted by her husband.

'You don't say?' retorted Beef, with his heaviest sarcasm. I might have known that he would not like his own credit being shared.

He adopted a somewhat stern demeanour when, later that evening, we again called at Mr Chickle's house to see Mrs Pluck. The old gentleman was still away, though he was expected to return on the following morning. Mrs Pluck grudgingly asked us in.

'I been to Pittenden,' announced Beef.

Still the woman tried to keep up her defensive shield of rudeness and indifference. Her face did not change at the mention of Pittenden.

'I'm sure I don't care where you've been,' she said.

'I've seen the register in the parish church.'

Now she was staring at him.

'So you know?' she gasped.

'I know that Shoulter was your husband.'

Just as once before we had found that behind her surliness were floods of loquacity which once released were hard to check, so we found ourselves now listening to a long disjointed colloquy.

'Well, it's true. I did marry him. But I never had anything to do with his murder, though I wouldn't have been sorry at that if you hadn't started nosing round and finding out who he was. Now I suppose my daughter'll get to hear of it and it's a shame, because she's no idea but what her father's dead. He was always a dirty rotter and what I married him for I can't think. It's plain why he married me – because he thought it was a nice little farm property for him to come into and live comfortable. Then, when he found out that the place was mortgaged and my father in a bad way and the little girl born, he went off. They told me I ought to have gone after him for the separation and put his picture in the newspapers and that, to find out where he was, but I wouldn't do that. Good riddance, I said, and knew I could manage as long as I didn't see his wicked face again. And I might never have done if I hadn't come to work here and heard the name Shoulter, and wondered if it was him. Then one day I ran into him in Barnford and he knew me at once, and after that there was no peace at all. He found out about Mabel getting married and everything, and started wanting money and saying if I didn't give it him he'd go over and tell her who he was, and that would have upset everything. I gave him what I had, and of course he wanted more. That's what I had to see Mabel about on Christmas Eve. I shall never forget young Ribbon coming in and saying he was lying dead up the footpath. I won't say I was sorry because I wasn't. It was a weight off my mind. And I'd never told anyone he was my husband and never thought you'd come along and find out and think I'd murdered him.'

'If you didn't,' said Beef, 'who did?'

'That's what I've been asking myself ever since I heard it was murder and not suicide. Well, I never thought it was suicide, really. He wasn't the kind for that. Thought too much about himself.'

'Do you think he was getting money from anyone else?'

'I don't see how he could have been, down here anyway. Unless his poor sister used to give him anything, which I doubt.'

'Did he have anything to do with Mr. Chickle?'

'So far as I know they never met.'

Beef seemed lost in thought. At last he spoke.

'I can't see why you don't tell your daughter and son-in-law the whole thing,' he said at last. 'Nice young chap. He'd understand all right. And so would she.'

Mrs Pluck made no answer to that, but she did concede before we left her that she 'supposed we had our job to do,' and I had the impression that she was happier for having got the story of her marriage off her chest. But that, I reflected, did not make her innocent.

CHAPTER TWENTY-FOUR

The Inevitable Second Corpse

THERE followed a day of inactivity for me, during which Beef did what he called 'studying his notes'. I have long since given up doing anything of the sort myself, for in reading other detective novels with the eye of an experienced chronicler I have come to the reluctant conclusion that lists of suspects, time-tables, elaborate catalogues of clues and so on are the resort of those who feel the need to fill another chapter when nothing in the way of true detection presents itself. Besides, I accept my task as that of relating the doings of Beef as faithfully as another author described 'What Katy Did', and I have decided not to vary from this rule. If my activities are of the least importance it may be said that I played a game of snooker at the Barnford Working Men's Club and waited for the results of the no doubt monumental deliberations that were being done by Beef.

'Solved it?' I asked cheerfully that evening.

'Not altogether. I can't see any reasonable motive.'

When I know that he is indulging in mysteriousness I leave him severely alone.

'Chickle came back to-day,' he observed.

'Indeed?'

'Yes. On the same train as Shoulter took that day.'

'Ah,' I said, mimicking his favourite interjection.

'We'll go up and see him in the morning.'

'Don't you think he may get rather tired of your visits?'

'I hope so,' said Beef enigmatically.

But we were destined to see Chickle before the morning, and in circumstances which, even to me, with my long experience of the unexpected, were astonishing.

At about ten to ten that evening, when I was rather unwillingly taking down the scores for a game of darts which

Beef was playing in the public bar, Mr Bristling came in and whispered to me that Mrs Pluck was in the bottle and jug and wanted to see Beef most particular. As soon as he had thrown the double-eighteen which he needed for a finish, Beef accompanied me and we interviewed the housekeeper in the little back room where Joe Bridge had told us his story. It was plain at once that she was in a state of great trepidation.

'Whatever's the matter?' asked Beef, to whom the visit was unwelcome, coming as it did so close to closing time.

'It's Mr Chickle,' she blurted out. 'He came home this afternoon looking ever so ill and funny. He didn't hardly speak to me and didn't eat a bite with his tea. Then as soon as it was dark he got on his coat and hat and said, "Mrs Pluck, I'm going to call on Mr Flipp, you understand. If anyone should want to know where I've gone you tell them I've gone to call on Mr Flipp. Don't forget that, please." And he marched off and hasn't come home since. It's the best part of five hours he's been gone and I'm worried sick, what with that murder in the wood and everything.'

'Did he take his gun?' asked Beef.

'His gun? Certainly not. Whatever for? It was dark when he started out.'

'Well, there's only one thing for it. We must go and report to Inspector Chatto and see what he says. I shouldn't be surprised but what he decides to go up to Mr Flipp's home. Come on.'

Neither Inspector Chatto nor Constable Watts-Dunton seemed very pleased to see us, but when he had heard Mrs Pluck's story the inspector decided, as Beef had anticipated, to go at once to 'Woodlands'. We waited only while the two policemen hastily pulled on greatcoats and then the four of us set out, while Mrs Pluck went to the home of her friend Mrs Wilks, saying that nothing would persuade her to go up to 'Labour's End' again that night.

I shall not easily forget that long walk through the dark and cold of a windy January night. The two policemen were ahead, talking a little between themselves, but saying

nothing to us, whose presence was made to seem on suffer-
ance. Beef was silent, too, and I was glad to be left to my
own thoughts, which were by no means calm. In spite of all
Beef's investigation of Mrs Pluck, the case seemed to centre
round the two contrasting men whom we should find at
'Woodlands': the big bluff Flipp and little talkative Chickle.
I formed no definite idea of what I thought had happened,
but I agreed with the serious view taken by the police of
Chickle's failure to return after so long an interval.

As we tramped along with the wind in our faces a figure
loomed up in the road ahead, and Inspector Chatto threw
the light of his torch on the approaching man. It was Joe
Bridge.

'Where are you coming from?' asked Chatto.

'My home. Going down to Barnford.'

'Have you met anyone on the way?'

'Not a soul.'

I knew this was not Bridge's quickest route, but I said
nothing. Again we were trudging on. For a few minutes
there was a half-break in the clouds and a dull moon shone,
but soon it was dark again. At last we reached the end of
the long drive which went up through the wood to Flipp's
lonely house, and turned in. We were sheltered from the
wind now and, except for the rattle of the bare boughs over-
head, the night was quieter.

When 'Woodlands' came in sight Chatto stopped, and the
four of us stared into the semi-darkness.

'Not a light in the place,' said Chatto.

'May have gone to bed. It's nearly eleven now.'

'Then we must wake 'em up. Come on.'

We walked slowly up to the front door, peering about us
as though we expected some movement in the night. The
windows were like squares of wet ink, dark and shining.

Not a dog barked.

Then we had a surprise. The front door was wide open
and we could catch a glimpse of a dark hall beyond. We
stood listening for a few minutes, but there was not a sound
of movement.

'Anyone at home?' called Chatto. Then louder, 'Anyone at home?'

I had an eerie feeling that someone in the dark house was listening and waiting – perhaps crouching in fear or standing behind the locked door of a bedroom.

'Where's the switch?' asked Chatto.

'There's no electric light,' Watts-Dunton told him.

Chatto's torch played over the hall. What we saw was commonplace enough – a hall table, coats hanging, a few umbrellas. Nothing seemed out of place. Chatto crossed to a door on the left and, flinging it open, again let his torch play over the interior. It was a small dining-room, I judged; and lying on a mat before the last red cinders of a fire was the body of a man.

'My God!' I whispered to Beef. 'That looks like Flipp!'

It was Flipp. He was prone on his stomach with his face buried in his arms, fully dressed. Chatto stooped over him.

'Is he dead?' I asked.

'Dead drunk,' was the curt reply, after the inspector had made a brief examination. 'Can't you smell it?'

There was, indeed, a stench of stale alcohol in the air.

Watts-Dunton struck a match and set it to the table lamp. A yellow light, inadequate though it was, made the figure on the floor discernible in greater detail. Chatto had turned him over now and I could see the almost purple face of the police suspect.

Without ceremony Chatto emptied a carafe of water over the man's head, and Flipp stirred, at first uneasily and then with a sudden jerk.

'What the hell . . .'

But before he could form his question Chatto snapped. 'Where's your wife?'

'Gone.' said Flipp, and fell back again.

'And the servants?'

'Gone. Everyone gone. Left me alone. Who the hell are you?'

'Police,' said Chatto.

This time Flipp sat up and attempted unsuccessfully to rise to his feet.

'What do you want?' he asked.

'I'm looking for Mr Chickle.'

Flipp seemed to lose interest. He said: 'Oh,' and closed his eyes.

'When did you see him last?'

'Who? Chickle? Days ago.'

'You haven't seen him to-day?'

'To-day? No. Haven't been out all day. Everyone gone and left me. No food – nothing. Wife deserted me. Servants flown. Now I want to sleep.'

Chatto shook him.

'We know positively that Mr. Chickle came to see you this evening.'

'Positively didn't.'

'He set off from his home with the object of seeing you.'

'Never – well – came here, I tell you. I know Chickle. If he'd come here I'd have seen him.'

'What time did you start drinking?'

'Thirty years ago.'

'Don't be funny, Mr Flipp. What time to-day did you start?'

'All day on and off. Wife deserted me. But I'm sober enough to see Chickle.'

'How long have you been asleep?'

'Few minutes. Dropped off about eight o'clock.'

Chatto indicated to Watts-Dunton with a nod that he should stay with Flipp. The rest of us started to search the house. It soon became clear to us that Flipp had spoken the truth when he said that his wife and servants had left him. In their rooms the cupboards and drawers had been emptied and a confusion of unwanted clothes and packing paper was left on the floor and furniture. But no one was in the house. We conscientiously looked in every space large enough to conceal a human being.

I found a large tin trunk in one bedroom and was proceed-

ing to prise it open when Beef asked what I expected to find
in it.

'Think Chickle's inside?' he asked grinning.

It was scarcely large enough to hold a man even of the
little watchmaker's size, so I asked Beef if he'd ever heard
of corpses being cut up. This must have flummoxed him, for
he laughed and walked on. The box was full of empty
bottles.

At last it was clear that we should have to look elsewhere
for Chickle, and we gathered in the hall.

'You'll have to stay here to-night,' said Chatto to Watts-
Dunton. 'I'll get a warrant out for Flipp first thing to-
morrow.'

Watts-Dunton returned to his charge and the three of us
went out again into the chilly and dismal night. It seemed
that the wind had dropped a little as we stood outside, or
else that the shelter of the trees produced a certain quiet-
ness. At all events I was conscious of night sounds – the hoot
of an owl and what sounded like a horse kicking the wooden
partition of his stall in the shed near which we were standing

Chatto was planning that we should go to 'Labour's End'
by the route which Chickle would have used when Beef
suddenly gave a signal for silence and said 'Ussh!'

We stood there looking at Beef and wondering what on
earth he had heard.

'Flipp hasn't got a horse, has he?'

'Shouldn't think so; why?'

'That's not a horse, anyway,' he said excitedly, and made
a bolt for the door of the shed near which we were standing.
It yielded to him, and by the light of Chatto's powerful
torch we gazed into the interior.

Has the reader guessed? If so he has more perspicacity
than I had, for to me the sight was utterly unexpected.
There were stout beams across the shed, no more than eight
feet from the ground. From the one of these nearest to a
partition was hanging the body of Wellington Chickle, his
feet beating the horrible tattoo which we had heard from

outside the door. Like Flipp he was fully dressed and wore a greatcoat, while his felt hat was ludicrously pulled over his eyes. An old wooden chair lay toppled at his feet as though he had kicked it away from under him.

In a moment Chatto had pulled out a claspknife and cut the rope while Beef lowered the little man to the ground. I waited breathlessly while Beef stooped over him.

'Dead as mutton,' was his vulgar and irreverent verdict when he had made his examination.

CHAPTER TWENTY-FIVE

Chatto gets his Warrant

FOR some moments we stared down at that grotesque little figure. Then Chatto threw the light of his torch on to a white square of paper roughly pinned to the left lapel of the coat and we read three words written in big childish letters: 'I have failed.' If this was suicide the dead man had chosen a singularly curt message, and I at once wondered why it was written in these big square letters when normal hand-writing would have served as well.

The crumpled body in its neat black clothes was not with-out pathos, I considered, though the protruding eyes and hideously stretched lips made it seem more macabre than pitiful. And I realized how little we knew of this urbane old man who was in some mysterious way bound up with the crime we were investigating, and who, according to his housekeeper, had changed so drastically since the afternoon of the murder.

'That settles it,' said Chatto curtly. 'If I'd had any doubts about arresting Flipp this would have been enough. Unless I'm very much mistaken this is Flipp's third murder.'

'Think so?' said Beef. 'What makes you think this is murder?'

'What else could it be but a murder meant to look like suicide?'

'It *could* be a suicide meant to look like murder,' asserted Beef.

Chatto made that interesting sound usually reproduced by novelists as 'Pshaw!'

Beef stooped over the corpse. 'You think this label was pinned on him?' he asked.

'I do,' Chatto told him.

'Well, here's a clue for you. If it was pinned on by another person he was left-handed.'

'How d'you make that out?'

'It's a little towards the left breast and the pin runs from left to right as you face Chickle or from right to left as he would handle it himself. Try handling a pin on yourself and then on someone else and see which way you instinctively put it.'

All our tempers, I think, were a trifle frayed, for it was nearing midnight and we were tired and anxious to be in warm beds

'And you seriously ask me to decide that Mr Chickle committed suicide because the pin on that label runs in that particular direction?' Chatto's voice was loud in exasperation.

'I don't ask you to decide anything. In fact what I'm doing is to suggest that you should *not* decide yet. You'd more than half made up your mind that it was murder.'

'I had. *And* I still think so. What's he doing here otherwise? We know he set out to see Flipp. It may be that while he was away he'd found out something about Flipp. Or it may be that he's known all along and suddenly decided to speak to Flipp. At all events he came here and found Flipp alone. We can guess what happened. It would not have been hard for that big fellow to have choked the life out of the poor little bloke, then strung him up in his shed and pinned that label on him and gone and got himself drunk.'

'All that *could* have happened,' admitted Beef. 'But I don't think it did. I'm interested in the words on that piece of paper – *I have failed*. They don't seem to me exactly the message that would be chosen by a murderer for his victim if he wanted it to look like suicide. There's something very real about them.'

Chatto ignored that and rather impatiently began to go through the dead man's pockets. Nothing. There was not even a handkerchief in them.

'That cuts both ways,' observed Beef.

'We'll lock this shed up and leave everything as it is till the morning. Then we'll get the medico out and have a proper examination. It's past midnight now and I'm not going to drag him out here to-night.'

The key was on the outside of the lock, so this was quite easy. But before leaving 'Woodlands' we crossed again to the house and found Constable Watts-Dunton sitting peacefully in a chair reading by the light of the oil lamp. Flipp was still lying on the floor breathing stertorously. Chatto called the constable out of the room and told him in a hurried whisper what we had found. The long, serious face of Watts-Dunton did not change as he heard it.

'I'll keep an eye on the shed till you all come up in the morning,' was all he said.

'Happen to know if anyone connected with this case is left-handed?' asked Chatto. I smiled to perceive that he had been more impressed by Beef's little argument than he had admitted at the time.

'I don't recall anyone. *He* wasn't,' he said with a contemptuous nod at the figure of Flipp. 'I know that because he once turned out for the cricket team. Nor's Bridge. He plays every week. Can't say about Mrs Pluck, of course.'

'Better wake him up. There's something I've got to ask him at once.'

This was not so easy as it sounded, but after a good deal of shaking from Watts-Dunton, Flipp eventually opened his eyes.

'What is it?' he asked drowsily.

'Have you been across to your mixing shed this evening?'

'Yes. Course I have. Fed the chickens. My wife's deserted me.'

'What time?'

'About four o'clock. Why?'

'Never mind why. All right, constable. We'll get along.'

I noticed that Flipp's head dropped back and his eyes closed automatically even before we had left the room.

We started the walk home with the wind behind us and were soon out on the road. We had not gone half a mile, however, when we heard someone whistling a tune ahead of us and recognized Joe Bridge. Chatto stopped him.

In the light of certain events of this evening about which you will doubtless hear later,' began Chatto, 'I'm afraid I must ask you where you have been, Mr Bridge.'

'All right. I've been to see my uncle in Barnford.'

'Funny time of night to pay a call.'

'Yes. Wasn't it? Good night,' returned Bridge cheerfully, and recommencing his whistling he strode on.

I was scarcely awake next morning before Beef was in my room saying that we had a job to do and adjuring me to jump into my clothes quick. I obliged him as far as I conveniently could though I would not renounce my shave. He led me off at a fast pace, and it was scarcely seven before he was knocking at the door of Mrs Wilks's cottage. I was relieved when the door was opened by Mrs Pluck.

'Something to tell you,' Beef mumbled.

'What is it now?'

'Mr Chickle's dead. Thought you'd better know at once.'

'Oh, my God. How?'

'Hanged.'

'You mean he hanged himself?'

'That or – well, the police think it may be murder.'

'Wherever's this going to stop?' cried Mrs Pluck. 'First one, then another.'

'It will stop when Shoulter's murderer is arrested. Now I want you to come up to Chickle's house. I want to have a good look round. He may have left something interesting.'

'All right. Wait here. I won't be a minute.'

Her prediction was almost accurate. In a very short time she had joined us, wearing the rusty black hat and coat she had had on when she had called at our inn on the previous night – which seemed an age ago to me. She proved herself the farmer's daughter we knew her to be on her way up to 'Labour's End', striding along ahead of us so that I was soon panting in my efforts to keep up.

Inside the bungalow she became the efficient housekeeper.

'I don't suppose you've either of you had a cup of tea, have you? Sit down while I get a kettle boiling. Poor old chap – I'm not surprised though. I told you he'd been funny lately and yesterday when he came in he looked right down queer.'

'You don't think it was murder then?'

'Who's going to murder *him*? The other one I could understand. But Mr Chickle was a kind little soul. Friendly word for everyone. I'm sure he hadn't an enemy in the world.'

We were soon drinking hot sweet tea and munching some bread and butter. Mrs Pluck seemed thoughtful, but not unduly distressed.

Then Beef made a systematic search of Chickle's room, turning out drawers and cupboards, and examining papers. He did not hurry, but he did not seem to find anything to interest him. Papers were arranged methodically and were not in any case abundant, so that the search took less time than I had anticipated. It was then extended to the rest of the house with as little result.

'You'd have thought he'd have left a letter, wouldn't you? He was that sort.'

By the time we had returned to Barnford the village was stirring and I saw a motor-cycle outside the police-station.

'Looks as though Chatto's got his warrant,' remarked Beef.

As we were finishing breakfast I decided to attempt the usually unprofitable business of pumping Beef on his theories and conclusions. He made his usual retort that I knew just as much as he did, so that my guess was as good as his.

'Do what your readers have learnt to do,' he suggested, 'and choose the least likely of the lot, then see where that gets you.'

'I suppose the least likely is Aston,' I suggested tentatively.

'What about the youth Ribbon?' grinned Beef.

'I hadn't thought of him.'

'Then there are Mrs Pluck and the two servants and Mabel Muckroyd...'

'I refuse to suspect her.'

'Why? It's been known to be ever such nice people before now.'

'You think you know who murdered Shoulter?' I asked.

'Yes. I think I do.'

'Then why don't you go to Chatto and tell him your theory?'

'Because it's not complete yet. I'll tell you one thing. As I see it, one of the keys to the whole thing is that little inscription *I have failed*. And another's that pair of outsize shoes. And another is the Christmas card which Miss Packham sent to Flipp.'

'Now you're only making it more difficult.'

'Well, it is difficult. I doubt if we shall ever prove the thing conclusively. It's an unusual case, as you'll realize.'

'Mm. You think Chatto's making a mistake?'

Beef grew more genial as the police were blamed.

'He's ignoring too much evidence,' he said. 'He chooses what suits his notions and leaves out what doesn't.'

Speak of the devil, I thought, for at that moment Inspector Chatto walked into the room. There was a considerable change in him since the previous night — he looked fresh and sleek and smoothly shaved, and he was smiling amiably.

'I thought you two would like to be there when I make the arrest,' he said. 'Since you've helped me with two or three little bits of evidence. I've got the warrant and I'm going up in a few minutes.'

'I should like it,' agreed Beef. 'It's always interesting to see how a man behaves when he's accused of murder.'

Chatto grinned.

'Especially when he's wrongly accused, eh? Well, come along the pair of you and you shall see for yourselves. I've got a police car this morning.'

We needed no second invitation. We pulled on our great-coats, for it was a bitterly cold morning, and followed the inspector out.

CHAPTER TWENTY-SIX

Mr Flusting Talks

FLIPP had sobered up and had had a wash and shave before we arrived at 'Woodlands'. Indeed, he looked a great deal fresher than Constable Watts-Dunton. He showed little surprise or emotion as Chatto brought out the whole portentous formula, ending with its warning that anything he said might be used in evidence against him.

'I thought you suspected me,' he remarked dully.

Chatto had read out all three of the names he had used, and although he took no apparent notice of the Philipson and Flipp, he asked, rather anxiously I thought, why Chatto had called him Phelps.

'Perhaps you've forgotten that,' said Chatto calmly. 'It was the name you used to sign the poison book in Shoulter's shop.'

I was watching the wretched man intently and saw that this quiet statement had had its effect.

'I want to see my solicitor – Mr. Aston,' he said, and there was a slight trembling noticeable.

'You can telephone for him from the police-station,' conceded Chatto. 'We're taking you over to Ashley.'

Watts-Dunton brought his coat, and Flipp made a great point of locking up the house. He was accompanied from door to door after he had carefully shut the windows from the inside. It was without further conversation, however, that we left 'Woodlands'.

That afternoon, in response to a telegram from Beef, there arrived at Barnford the last of the many people we had to meet in this case. Recalling it now I have to admit that I could see no point in sending for Mr Flusting, that friend of Chickle's who had been mentioned more than once in the course of our investigation. He had been quoted as a lifelong friend of the little watchmaker who had been a neighbour of his during all the years in which Chickle had built up his thriving business. But I could not see how he would throw any light either on the murder of Shoulter or on the death of Chickle himself. Beef, however, set great store on the talk he would have with Mr Flusting, and even spoke of the 'last link in the chain'.

He arrived at Barnford by the now fateful train, and Beef was on the station to meet him. He was a tall, thin, grey-haired man who wore old-fashioned rimless pince-nez, a black overcoat and a starched collar too large for his thin neck. His eyes were blue and rheumy and he spoke in a high-pitched voice which he attempted to modulate into a tone of solemnity in speaking of the dead man.

'Thought you ought to know at once,' said Beef as we walked away from the station.

Mr Flusting's next words surprised me.

'Suicide, I suppose?' he said. It was clear that he saw nothing inconsistent in this.

'That's what I think it is,' said Beef. 'But the police have other ideas.'

'No, no. Suicide, I'm afraid. In fact, I will go so far as to say I saw it coming.'

'Did you indeed?'

'Yes. He has just been to see me, you know. Stayed a few days. He was very far from normal, Sergeant. Very far from it.'

Beef did not want to hurry Mr Flusting into any sketchy talk, I thought, but was determined to have the whole story from him in detail.

'Suppose we go and have a cup of tea,' he suggested. 'And you tell me what you can? You see, Mr Flusting, I'm of the opinion that your knowledge of the dead man will be of the greatest assistance to us in clearing up the mystery surrounding these two deaths. I don't know the police opinion on that, but I know mine. And if you would be so good as to tell us what you knew of Mr Chickle, both in the past and more recently, it would be very valuable.'

'I'll certainly tell you all I can,' replied Mr Flusting. 'But

I have begun to wonder lately whether I really knew Chickle at all. There were depths in that man ...'

'Not another word till you've had a cup of tea,' exclaimed Beef as we arrived at the Crown.

But the time came for Flusting to talk. He lit his pipe, looked weakly at the pair of us and began:

'I've known Wellington Chickle since he was a youth,' he announced, 'and apprenticed to a watchmaker. And I don't think that anyone else has known him at all. There were two of him, you know, the bland and commonplace shop-keeper, and behind that façade a fiery and ambitious soul who was determined to leave his mark on the world. That is the thing you must understand about him – the key to the whole character of the man – he was determined to leave his mark on the world. It may seem odd if you think only of the chatty little man you probably knew, but remember I have seen behind all that. I have heard his deepest confidences. From the very first that was his resolve.'

'And how did he go about doing it?'

'For many years, oddly enough, in the most conventional way. He meant to build up a big business, make money and I suppose achieve success in the most ordinary manner. Perhaps he saw himself as a J.P., a Mayor, or a Member of Parliament, and in one of these offices making history. At any rate, for nearly all the years of our friendship he dedicated himself to increasing his business and making a fortune, and as you probably know he was successful in both. So successful that when the time came for him to sell his business and retire he was a rich man. I think one might say a very rich man. It was then that he gave me his first surprise.'

'What was that?' asked Beef.

'Well, I was waiting to see what he would do next. I knew that he must do something. He wasn't old. He had a vigorous mind and body. It was the moment for him to put into practice those secretly nourished ambitions of his. I wondered whether he would start by buying a newspaper or a title. He had once confided in me in all solemnity that a

teacher at his school had told him that he would never set
the Thames on fire, and that he was going to show him
something that would astonish him. Now was the time.
What form would it take?'

We both stared at Mr Flusting as he asked this rhetorical
question.

'To my amazement,' went on Mr Chickle's old friend, 'he
did nothing. After selling the business he moved into rooms
in London and remained there, apparently in aimless con-
tentment. I could not understand it. I even ventured to
query this, but all I got was a series of mysterious nods and
winks and hints that he had something up his sleeve. But I
could not help wondering what that something might be.
And as time went on and he made no move and seemed
content to live the rest of his days as an obscure retired
watchmaker, I was more and more puzzled.

'Then he gave me the biggest surprise of all. He
announced that he had purchased a bungalow in the country and was going down there to live quietly and grow roses.
I could not believe it. You must understand that to no one
else would it seem strange, but to me, who knew the inner
secrets of Wellington Chickle, it was incredible. Frankly, I
remonstrated. I asked him what had happened to all his
ambitions, the determination he had long ago voiced to me
to leave his mark on the world. All he did was to smile.
"There are more ways than one of doing that," he said. I
should see.

'What was I to think? Was he going to grow an immortal
rose like the American station-master in *Mrs Miniver*?
Or was he, could he possibly be, writing a book? Had he
some scheme of achieving undying fame like Gilbert White
of Selborne? It was difficult to believe, for whatever else he
was, he was not literary. I decided not to press him for
information, but simply to wait and see what my peculiar
little friend would do.

'For his first year here he seemed cheerful and busy
enough, except when he heard that the man who had
bought his business had dared to change its name. That

upset him. After all, whatever he was planning now the only thing he *had* achieved was his name in two-foot gilt letters over a flourishing shop. And that they should be erased so soon, to make way for a stranger's, really distressed him.

'However, it made the hints he gave me more frequent. There was something almost sly in the way he spoke of himself. And frankly for the first time I began to wonder whether my old friend could be considered quite sane. I had always thought his secret intention to astonish the world was a sort of *idée fixe*, you know, and dangerously near to a monomania, but now I considered the matter more seriously.

'Then came this murder down here which seemed to upset him altogether. I would never have believed he was human enough to feel it so deeply, and as far as I know he had never spoken to the victim. But from the very day after it he became a changed man, and when he came to stay with me last week I knew that in some way which I could not understand he was heartbroken. He told me, in so many words, that he had failed.'

'In what?' asked Beef.

'That he never explained. I was left to suppose that it was in Life, in Everything, and that something had just happened to make him realize it.'

'But it might have been in some particular thing?' queried Beef.

'It might have, but I can't see in what. Unless he had really been writing a book and had realized that he could not finish it, or that no one would publish it. But I cannot describe to you the state of depression he was in while he was with me. I who knew him well had never seen him anything but cheerful. Complacent might be a better word. Or self-satisfied. But now he was another man. He spoke most bitterly, again and again reiterating that all his schemes had failed. And when I received your telegram this morning I was not in the least surprised. In fact, he had even hinted that he did not want to continue living.'

'Did he give you the impression of being afraid of something?' Beef asked.

'No. I can't say he did. It was not fear. It was frustration. Anger, even. Disappointment. But I don't think fear. Why? Was there anything in the manner of his death to suggest that? Or did he leave a note of any kind?'

Beef told him of the curt wording which had been on the paper affixed to his coat.

'Ah, yes,' said Mr Flusting. 'That sounds like him. He used the very phrase to me a dozen times. That is what he felt – that he had failed. No doubt we shall soon know exactly how.'

'No doubt we shall,' said Beef.

'You say the police think that it's murder?'

'I believe so. They arrested the man they suspected of Shoulter's murder and it seems they believe him to be guilty of both. But it's only fair to say that they have scarcely begun investigating Mr Chickle's death. They may completely change their minds.'

'It was suicide, I feel sure,' said Mr Flusting earnestly, his Adam's apple jumping like a cork. 'He was *not* himself, Sergeant Beef. Not in the least. I would even go so far as to use the word insane.'

For the first time Beef grinned.

'Would you now? That's interesting.'

'Yes,' said Mr Flusting, 'I would. Or if not actually insane, certainly most abnormal. I feared it might come. Vaulting ambition, you know. I often think we more ordinary folk are lucky. We ask far less. We are more easily made up. That little old friend of mine had a tormented soul.'

I remembered the words afterwards. 'A tormented soul.'

'Well,' said Beef, bringing our visitor to earth. 'You'll be wanted at the inquest, I expect.'

Mr Flusting sighed.

'I suppose so,' he said.

CHAPTER TWENTY-SEVEN

Chatto States his Case

THAT evening we held the last conference in what was called in the Press the 'Deadman's Wood Murder Case'.

Chatto, very pleased with himself and twinkling with good humour, told us that since Beef had given him more than one piece of valuable information, he was going to let him in on the case against Flipp as the police had formulated it. As he outlined it to us in the little back parlour of the Crown, where so much had come to light during our investigations, I could not help feeling the strength of it. I was convinced that whatever Beef might have up his sleeve there was little doubt that Flipp would hang.

'I'm not going over the murder of his wife and I don't know what view the prosecuting counsel will take of that,' said Chatto. 'Nor am I going to try to prove Flipp guilty of murdering Chickle – though personally I believe he did so – for the simple reason that we have not got enough evidence yet. I'm going to concentrate on the murder of Shoulter, about which I cannot see that there can be any doubt at all. If I prove *that*, the murder of his wife goes with it, as far as I can see, and it's more than likely that the murder of Chickle follows.

'First of all, what brought Flipp to live at Barnford? The Shoulters. Then either he was friendly with Shoulter or, as we maintain, he was being blackmailed by him. The latter is virtually a certainty, and I don't think that Flipp himself will deny it, though he will probably maintain that he never administered poison to his wife but was being blackmailed by Shoulter because he had purchased morphine at that time and was afraid that if this were known a case would be made against him. At all events there was the poison book with his signature hidden in Shoulter's room, there were the withdrawals of money from his account in notes of

small denominations, withdrawals which were made before
Shoulter's visits to Barnford, and his calls on Flipp after
dark. Surely very little doubt about the blackmail?'

'Very little,' conceded Beef.

'Right. Then we have this powerful man of violent temper
who had already, we believe, despatched one human being
who stood in his way, being bled by a drunken ne'er-do-well
who was in all probability the *only* man who had the information on which Flipp was being blackmailed. The set-
up is pretty plain, isn't it? Moreover Flipp had a gun and
cartridges of a type used by half a dozen people in the
neighbourhood; Flipp knew that Shoulter was coming down
for Christmas and would walk alone through Deadman's
Wood. What could be more obvious?

'What is more, Flipp knew that there were at least two
people in Barnford on whom suspicion might fall, and there
was a very good chance of at least one of them not having
an alibi that afternoon. There was the retired watchmaker,
Chickle, and the hot-tempered young farmer, Joe Bridge.
Now he himself had noticed and called attention to the fact
that little Chickle was very fond of a particular spot on the
footpath through the woods which Shoulter would have to
pass. Why not, then, lay in wait for him there? If Shoulter
was shot in a place which Chickle, in Mr. Townsend's word,
haunted, and Chickle was known to carry such a gun as
Shoulter was shot with, there was a reasonable chance of
Chickle being suspected, however improbable Chickle's
action might seem. Again he knew that it was Joe Bridge's
custom to walk down to Barnford from Copling on Saturday
afternoons to see his uncle and aunt, and with any luck this
would bring the farmer to the spot. All he had to do was to
approach it by a route through the wood itself from his
house, wait for Shoulter to appear, shoot him, and return
home without being seen.

'Then, like all murderers, he over-plotted. His wife was
away for Christmas and it suddenly appeared to him that at
all costs the servants must be got away from "Woodlands",
in case they saw too much of his movements. This is where

he made his first mistake. As it happened the girls were not keen on going and he *insisted*. Now why? What possible reason could he have for insisting on their absence unless he wished to remain unobserved? To my mind that alone was almost enough to hang him.

'But he left further evidence. We know beyond doubt — and we owe the knowledge to you, Beef — that he was in the wood that afternoon, and not many yards from the place where the crime was committed. Miss Packham had sent him a Christmas card which was delivered to him shortly before three. He was already dressed to go out — in an old mackintosh which, as we also know from Beef, had a pocket-lining missing. The card was handed to him, he hurriedly stuffed it into his pocket, for he had not much time to spare, and subsequently dropped it on his way to the clearing. It was found there by a Boy Scout.

'Moreover we know from Miss Shoulter that in spite of Flipp's statement that he *never left his house* he was *not* in fact there when she called at three-forty-five. He was, as a matter of fact, on his way back from the clearing where he had just killed Shoulter.

'And lastly there is Joe Bridge's statement that as he approached the clearing a man in a raincoat was slinking away through the trees. If this was not Flipp, who else could it have been? Not Chickle, for Bridge described him as a biggish man. There is no one else possible, unless you are going to suppose that some complete stranger of whom we haven't heard was waiting for Shoulter in the wood that day. The only two other males in the district who are known to go into that wood at all are the poacher Fletcher and Packham the parson. Neither of them possesses a raincoat. No, I think you can take it that Flipp was standing among the trees waiting for Shoulter to come from the direction of Barnford when he heard someone, who turned out to be Bridge, coming from the direction of Copling. Not wishing to be seen, he hurried off among the trees to return when Bridge had gone. Right?'

'Right!' said Beef with an emphatic nod.

'Then, as we know from Bridge, Shoulter came up the path a few minutes later, since Bridge met him before he reached Chickle's bungalow half a mile away. *And he was carrying his golf-clubs*. What, I should like to know, was in that bag? In my theory it was the gun which he had borrowed without permission from his sister some weeks before. After he had killed his blackmailer Flipp may have noticed this and it gave him an altogether new idea. Why should not this be made to appear suicide? It would be yet another fortified line in his own defence.

'Flipp's failing as a murderer was to overdo things. If he had been satisfied with having left the suspicion to fall on Chickle or Bridge he would have made his case a better one. But no – he could not resist this new idea. He pulled the corpse to the side of the clearing so that it would not be visible from the path and with the only kind of line handy – a length of red tape which was either in his pocket or Shoulter's – he rigged it as best he could to look as though Shoulter had shot himself. Clumsy that. It scarcely needed our ballistics expert to say that the man had been shot from some yards away while he was on the footpath. In defence of Flipp's intelligence it must be remembered that the face of a man shot at point-blank range by a twelve-bore would have been so nearly shot away that at the time he could scarcely be expected to see that a ballistics expert would be able to gauge the exact distance of the barrel from the head.

'Just as his arrangements were complete, some time past four o'clock he realized that he was making a serious mistake. *The gun by the dead man had not been fired*. Still wearing his gloves he remedied this, using two of his own cartridges. Then he returned stealthily to "Woodlands", quite unaware that Miss Shoulter had been there to see him, or that he had dropped the Packhams' Christmas card near the scene of the crime. He believed, in fact, that he had achieved a pretty clever murder.

'Now the rest is conjecture, I admit, and at present forms no part of our case, though I hope it will do so. For I believe that Flipp murdered Chickle. Why? And why, according to Chickle's housekeeper, was he so changed after that particular afternoon? There is only one answer that I can see — Chickle knew too much. He saw some part of the proceedings, perhaps the most fateful part. And it worried him. A peaceful little man of regular habits, he was distressed by being brought into contact with anything so violent, and was determined to keep out of it. He lied to us to save himself not from the dock but from the witness box — a form of lying more common than you would suppose. But it got on his mind. He grew, as Mrs Pluck said, distressed and unhappy. If he had only done his duty and told us what he knew he would have saved his life. But he preferred to keep it to himself. Well, you have seen the result. Flipp knew that he knew. They may even have talked together in that clearing over the body of the dead man. That we shall never know. At all events Flipp was taking no chances. He induced Chickle to come up to his house when no one else was there and silenced him for ever.'

'Wasn't that a bit clumsy?' suggested Beef. 'Hanging him in his own stable, I mean?'

Chatto shrugged his shoulders.

'This one *was* to look like suicide. And take in the other too. For if Chickle committed suicide it would appear that it was because he had in fact been a murderer. We know that Flipp was a gambler. He was getting odds of two-to-one. He would clear himself of *both* murders by this, or hang for the two. It wasn't a bad idea, as murderers' ideas go.

'Well, there you have it — lock, stock, and — appropriately enough — barrel. And I'm only waiting for you, Beef, to act according to precedent, pull the whole thing to pieces, and indicate an entirely different person as the murderer. Then Mr Townsend will be happy, the police will be made to look silly, and Mr Townsend's readers will get what they bargained for — a surprise in the last chapter. What about it?'

Beef shook his head.

'Can't do that,' he said. 'Can't pull it all to pieces. You've got too much truth there for me to treat your theory as a pack of cards.'

Both Chatto and I were startled, but for different reasons:

'Great Scott!' cried Chatto. 'You're not going to admit that the police are *right*?'

'Beef,' I exclaimed, 'if you let me down after all the time I have spent on this case and the writing I have already done, I shall consider it unforgivable. Are you going to sit there and tell me that the police suspect is guilty, and that you haven't got a theory after all?'

Beef chuckled in his most irritating way.

'Hadn't you both better wait till you've heard what I've got to say? I only said there was truth in what we've just heard. And there is. Any amount of truth. But what I don't like about it is that it leaves so much unaccounted for. If you don't mind my saying so, Inspector, you've *chosen* your bits of evidence to suit your theory. And I don't believe in doing that. I like a theory which covers *all* the evidence, not bits here and there. It's not to say that you aren't right enough in most of what you say. But what about Miss Shoulter's old shoes? And the shot at six-fifteen? And what Bridge saw Chickle doing in his garden? And the marks the Boy Scouts found on the tree? There's an awful lot you don't account for.'

'I thought this was coming,' said Chatto. 'Go on. You'd better tell us. Whom do *you* suspect?'

Beef sucked his moustache.

'I shall have to tell you the story in my own way,' he said.

Chatto leaned back in his chair.

'Go ahead,' he invited.

CHAPTER TWENTY-EIGHT

Beef Spills the Beans

'I FIRST began to take an interest in Mr Wellington Chickle,' announced Beef portentously, 'when I found him reading one of Townsend's books. I thought there must be something funny about a man that would do that for pleasure. And when I examined his library and found that every book in it was about crime I was certain that I was on to something. Not just crime novels, mind you, but legal books and technical books that could only be of interest, anyone would think, to a detective, a criminal lawyer, or a murderer.'

Beef paused and stared at each of us in turn, as though to mark the effect of his words. On Chatto this was practically nil. I felt a little pardonable irritation.

'Then there was his name. That struck me as peculiar. I mean, you just fancy going through life with a name like that. Think of the kids at school. And the fellows you'd meet later. Nothing short of cruel to send a lad through life with a label tagged on to him that was enough to make a laughing-stock of him. You never know what effect it will have either. I don't go much on psychology and that, but if half of what I've read is true, the name Wellington Chickle's enough to give a man a neurosis, a couple of fixations, and half a dozen complexes. And in this case it worked out a treat.

'All the same, though I noticed these two things about Mr Chickle, and a lot more later which I'll tell you about, all of which seemed to point to him in connexion with the crime, I was stumped for one thing. And that was a thing which you had very strongly for your suspect, Inspector. A motive. I could not see what possible reason this little man with the funny name could have for bumping off a fellow who, to the best of my knowledge and belief, was a complete stranger to him. Not, that is, until yesterday, when I met his lifelong friend and heard a lot about him which I'd only suspected before. He had a motive, but it was one of the queerest ones I've ever heard for a crime.'

Beef became irritatingly silent till Chatto prompted him.

'Have you ever heard of Art for Art's sake?' Beef went on at last. 'Well, that's what Wellington Chickle's idea was – murder for murder's sake. What he wanted to do was to kill someone. No one in particular. Just anyone. You heard what Flusting said? He meant to leave his mark on the world. And into his distorted little mind had come the idea that the surest way to do this was to commit a murder. Madness? Well, yes, if you like. But to my mind anyone who wants to leave his mark on the world's a madman, however he proposes to do it. This was just worse than others.

'That's where Flusting's story was valuable. I could not see that Chickle could have had any reason for planning Shoulter's death. And the answer was that he had not. He hadn't planned Shoulter's death, but the death of the first man who came down that path that afternoon. But let's get back to the beginning and see what he *did* plan, and how it all happened.

'The key to the whole thing is that Chickle decided, I think more than a year ago, to commit a murder. You must give me that or else what I'm going to tell you doesn't mean anything. He had retired from business with a nice bit of money to last him the rest of his days. And he wanted to do something that would have made a name for him. He might have gone into politics and no harm done. Or he might have took up some hobby and got himself famous. Instead of that he decided to go in for murder. Well, tastes differ. One man's drink is another man's poison, as you might well say.

'He admitted to me that he'd been down to Barnford years ago and probably remembered that footpath through the woods as a likely place. He soon found the ideal spot, but what does the crazy little fellow do but start practising – dodging down behind the fallen tree and that and looking a proper fool when the parson comes on him at his tricks, besides putting ideas into Flipp's head. But he hasn't yet thought out how he'll do it and he's just playing with the idea of a gun when Miss Shoulter asks him slap out if he likes shooting, and he's told a lie before he knows where he is. He wasn't very clever, really, you know. Thought he was, no doubt. Big ideas of himself as a murderer who would never be found out. But he made some stupid slips.

'Then he came round to the idea of a gun, rented the bit of shooting in Deadman's Wood, and made a habit of walking about there with a twelve-bore. His reason was obvious. When the day came and he used his gun, if he was seen it would be no more than his everyday habit. No one would think nothing about it.

'I think he made a mistake, just as you think Flipp made a mistake, in planning to make it look like suicide. That was just adding complications where none were needed. If he had just shot his man, any man, and relied on the absolute absence of any motive to clear him, and not started larking about with red tape and that, he'd have been better off. Because as soon as he decided to make it look like suicide he was up against the problem of a gun. He could not leave his own gun beside the dead man. So he decided to pinch that old one of Edith Shoulter's which always stood in a corner of the hall. Wasn't difficult, of course. Since he'd got everyone in the habit of seeing him *with* a gun. All he had to do was to go to the house one day without one and come away with it. Which he did.

'Then he would need a cord of some kind with which the dead man would have been supposed to have pulled the trigger of the gun with his foot — the usual method of suicides who shoot themselves. He was careful enough to realize that it was just such a thing as a piece of cord that gives murderers away, so he hit on the idea of red tape and stole a spool of it from the nearest lawyer's office.

'Finally there was a shot which had to be heard when he had a clear alibi. The shot which was actually to kill his man was easy enough, he would innocently say that he had taken a pot at a rabbit. But the shot that was to be *supposed* to be the fatal one was a different matter. He had to fix that. And it was only luck, really, that I got on to the way he done that – just young Bridge happening to notice him tying his garden line on to a line going off into the wood, and Mrs Pluck mentioning that he was out on the lawn *getting in his measuring line* when she heard the shot at six-fifteen. You notice, too, that whereas Chickle spoke of it as far off in the wood, she was positive it was close at hand. And Edith Shoulter who heard the other shots never noticed this one at all, so far from her house was it. In fact it was in the tree which the Scouts found.

'But there was what seemed like some luck with Chickle, too, during the days in which he was preparing for his crime. That pair of shoes of Edith Shoulter's which she sent to the Jumble Sale. He seized *that* opportunity at once. I was certain it was he who had worn the shoes, because Mrs Pluck noticed the change in him *from the time he came in from his walk* that day. He had obviously had the shock. Yet none of his footprints approached the clearing. Even if he wasn't guilty, how could he have *known* that there was anything wrong if he hadn't worn those shoes to go to the clearing? And we know that they had passed into his possession. This was later confirmed when I told him that the Boy Scouts were going to search the woods next day and he went out to recover the shoes from their hiding-place and tried to drop them out of sight when he saw us approaching. When he had had time to realize that I knew what he was carrying, he told another lie and said that they were an interesting find of his by the side of the path during his evening constitutional – at nearly midnight on a dirty wet night.

'It was pretty carefully planned, wasn't it?' said Beef, as though Wellington Chickle's preparations were a matter for his, Beef's, personal pride.

'M'm,' said Chatto.

'You see your theory doesn't really account for a good many things, does it?'

'What do you expect me to do then?' asked Chatto. 'Release Flipp, or charge him with the murder of his wife, and pin the murder of Shoulter on Chickle?'

Beef suddenly stood up and answered with all the emphasis he could command.

'Not without you want to make the biggest bloomer ever you made in your life!' he almost shouted.

'But you've just been proving Chickle's guilt....'

'I've just been proving that Chickle set out that afternoon to commit a murder. And I still say so. The nasty, half-crazy, conceited little jack-in-the-box meant to kill the first person as he came down that footpath. There was only one thing stopped him.'

'And that?'

'It had been done already, see? He'd come on a real murder. I was almost going to say a man's murder. A murder which had had a motive to it and been done against a blackmailer by his victim. As he walked up the path he came smack on the body of Shoulter whom Flipp had killed half an hour before.'

'So I *was* right,' gasped Chatto.

'Of course you was right in thinking Flipp had done it. Only you'd got the rest of it boxed up. When Chickle saw that, and right in the very spot where he had been going to do it, it gave him a nasty turn. For one thing he didn't know but what he might be suspected more when he hadn't done it than when he had. And he decided to carry out his original plan and fix up a suicide. As he had planned it he no doubt meant to get his victim near his gun-barrel by some trick, so that no expert in the world couldn't have told but what the dead man hadn't leaned over his own gun. He could only hope that the real murderer had done the same. By the look of what was left of Shoulter's head, he certainly had. Anyway he chanced it. He dragged the body to the fallen log and carried out his plan with the gun he had taken from Edith Shoulter and the tape he'd got from Aston's office, fired off the gun and went home to tea. At least, he'd said to himself, it was a stranger. You can

imagine what a shock it was to him that evening when
young Jack Ribbon came in and said it was Edith Shoulter's
brother. Of course he'd never seen him, but it brought the
thing rather to his doorstep.'

I put in a question.

'What makes you so sure of this?' I asked Beef. 'How can
you tell for certain that it wasn't Chickle who committed
the murder as well as faking the suicide?'

'Times, for one thing. Bridge saw Flipp at the clearing at
about three to three-fifteen. He passed Shoulter a few
minutes later and heard a shot, presumably from the clearing, a few minutes later still. If that wasn't the shot which
killed Shoulter it means that Shoulter sat waiting at the
clearing for an hour till Chickle came to shoot him at four-
fifteen. And that's silly. There were only three pairs of
shots. Those by which Shoulter was murdered at three-
fifteen say, those by which the gun was made to look as
though it had been used for suicide at about four-fifteen or
four-thirty, and those which we know came from Chickle's
contrivance in the tree soon after six. Now when the first
shots were fired Chickle was still in his garden. Bridge saw
him there. So he could not have done it. Simple, isn't it?

'Besides, there's another matter. From that afternoon on-
wards Chickle became depressed, and frequently said that
he had "failed". Why? Precisely because he *had* failed. He
found he could not even commit a murder. It smashed his
rotten little ego altogether, until at last he wrote *I have
failed* on a piece of paper and hanged himself in Flipp's
stables. Flipp's, mind you. Flipp was the man the police
suspected, the man whom Chickle either knew or guessed to
be guilty, and therefore the man who had done Chickle out
of his murder and the man whom he hated most. So if he
could do him a bit of harm he wanted to. "I'm going to Mr
Flipp's", he told his housekeeper twice, and went up there.

'It's imagination you need, Townsend,' went on Beef as
he eyed me solemnly. 'Imagination. You've got to be able to
put yourself even in the place of a little rat like Chickle if
you want to know what he'll do next. It's no easy task some-

times. But it's very often how I work my cases out. Imagination and plenty of common sense, and you can't go far wrong in detection.'

There was another long silence, which Beef at last broke. 'Quite satisfied?' he asked us.

Chatto for his part said frankly that Beef had done a fine piece of work. I was less easily pleased.

'It's all very well,' I grumbled. 'But you know what's expected of you – a big surprise in the last chapter. I can see that you've done well in tumbling to Wellington Chickle, but when all's said and done, whom do you point out as the guilty man? The one the police have suspected all along!'

Beef grinned.

'Well?' he said. 'You wanted a surprise, didn't you? And I don't know what this is, if it isn't one. The police "suspect" guilty! It's never been known to happen before in all the history of detective fiction. He's the one man that the most hardened reader never suspects. You're safe this time, my lad. You write it up and see.'

He laboriously stood up and stretched himself.

'Well, I don't know about you gentlemen,' he said. 'But I'm going to have a tumble down the sink. I think I've deserved it. Four pints please, Mr Bristling.'

'None for me, thanks,' said Constable Watts-Dunton primly.

'That's all right then,' said Beef irrepressibly. 'I can manage yours. Cheer-o, everyone.'

With an expert fist he tilted his tankard.

THE END